DIRTY
Jersey

Phillip Thomas Duck

DIRTY Jersey

KIMANI
tru
™

DIRTY JERSEY

ISBN-13: 978-0-373-83094-7
ISBN-10:   0-373-83094-7

www.kimanipress.com

Printed in U.S.A.

Acknowledgments

I give honor and thanks to the Creator, from whom all blessings flow, the alpha and the omega, the beginning and the end. God, thank you for my talent and blessings. Thank you for my drive and vision. Thank you. Thank you.

To my daughter, Ariana, thank you for your unbridled love and innocence.

To my mother, Melissa, thank you for your unwavering support and love. One day I'll try my best and give you back all I owe you tenfold. To my brother, Michael, thank you, and as always good things soon come. To my Uncle Joe, thanks. Uncle Pat, thank you. My aunts Jackie and Janice, thank you, love you both. Aunt Dorothy, RIP, you passed during the writing of this novel. I'm heartbroken and miss you much. My cousin Vern (my twin) and his lovely wife, Vanessa, much love. To my little cousins Jasmine, Andrew and Brianne, I thought of you all with each page I wrote. Thanks for the inspiration. And to the rest of my large and loving family, I can't count you each by number but I love you all with my heart and soul.

GGB (Gary Garfield Birch) and Pook (Wendell Logan), my brothers from a different mother. Your friendships are greatly appreciated. And yeah, we need to hang more, I know. My goddaughter, Elania, the only little girl as beautiful as my own. STA, you know who you are (smile), TOY always. Keith Lee Johnson (they need to build a Steak 'n Shake in the Dirty Jersey, bruh. What's going on? Lol.). Margaret Johnson-Hodge (My Literary Momma, thanks).

My agent, Sara Camilli, thanks.

My editor, Evette Porter. Getting this novel out of me was like pulling teeth, I know. I'm sorry the process was so painful, but I'm thankful you are so gifted and kind. Thank you. Thank you.

Linda Gill, thanks once again for the support and belief.

My writer family, keep pen to pad fam. What we do isn't easy, but it's enjoyable.

Pilgrim Baptist Church, Reverend Terrence K. Porter, thank you for the spiritual food.

To all the book clubs and groups, thanks for the support all these years.

I know I missed someone. Charge it to my head and not my heart.

Lastly, but certainly not least...my readers. Thank you. Holla at your boy in the "Dirty Jersey"—phillwrite@aol.com.

One,

Phillip Thomas Duck

I'm thinkin' why would I send you
when I knew it ain't right
I'm thinkin' what would
make you sacrifice ya life
You must love me

—Jay-Z, "You Must Love Me"

Eric

A fight, a fight
A black and a white
If the black don't win
We all jump in...

A dollop of sweat drips off the tip of my nose. It's so large and so heavy I swear I hear it as it thuds against the pavement. And that's saying something, because the pounding of my heart fills my eardrums like the bass line from a Timbaland song. I have my hands balled in a fist and up by my chin, in my boxing stance, my weight evenly distributed on the balls of my feet.

I'm ready to do some serious damage.

Across from me, Benny Sedgwick has his hands similarly fisted, but he holds them carelessly down at his sides. His greasy, unkempt hair keeps falling into his eyes, and he keeps swinging his head to clear it away and concentrate his focus on me. Benny's cheeks are beet red, his ocean-blue eyes wide as a big city highway. Acne dots his chin, his cheeks and forehead. The same hateful kids that tease me, they have a name for him as well: Pizza Face.

Benny and I have been friends for as long as I can remember. We've been one another's ally, one another's support system. A bonding of the uncool, I guess you could say. I just know he's wondering why I want to leave my knuckle prints tattooed on his face over all that acne. He's got to be wondering why I would want to hurt him.

I have to wonder myself.

"Come on, Poser," a too-deep-for-high-school voice calls from over my shoulder, "drop this fool-ass white boy so we can bounce."

Wonder no more.

That's Crash. His mother named him Percival Marques Johnson at birth, but if you want to know how he picked up the nickname Crash, then make the mistake of calling him by his "government name." I've seen Crash turn men into blubbering boys and boys into groaning girls for calling him Percival. Even most of the teachers at our high school are down with the program. Crash is feared by just about everyone. He's the only boy in our school with a tattoo. *Quod me nutrit me destruit*—"What nourishes me also destroys me." It's inked on his stomach. Drawn in among the ripples of his six-pack abs. It was there at the beginning of this school year, something Crash picked up over summer recess. I'm not even sure he knows what that Latin phrase means. I'd never say that to Crash, though. He'd destroy me if I did.

Benny, mindful of the heavy pull Crash has over me, attempts to talk me down off the ledge. "I was just fooling with Kenya," Benny whines. "Eric, you know that. Come on. Why are you taking this so serious?"

"Nah, nah, kill that noise," Crash says from behind me. "This white boy told your sister—a fine young Black Queen—to back that thing up. He disrespected the black woman, Poser. And not just any ol' bird, either. Your sister, B. I know you ain't takin' that, my dude."

I was in the lunchroom when it all happened. Kenya didn't appear too bothered by Benny's remark, to tell you the truth. In fact, she put her hands on her knees and morphed into the girl in Juelz Santana's "Clockwork" video. Sad to say, but my sister shook that behind like clockwork.

Not exactly the move of a disrespected Black Queen.

Crash says, "Enough of this. Bust this kid up, Poser. Bust him up."

Crash's voice has gotten even deeper. He's serious. Very serious.

I know Kenya's my sister. And her honor definitely means something to me. But Benny didn't mean anything by his remark, I'm certain of that. I want to explain all of this to Crash, but there is no explaining anything to him when his mind is set on something. He speaks, people listen. Period. End of story. A point that is not open for negotiation. Those who have tried to negotiate with Crash before have learned quickly, and usually painfully, the error of such a move. I don't want to be in that number.

"See, I'm about to get agitated," Crash says. "You ain't moving fast enough, Poser."

I grind my jaws then and manufacture the evilest look I can on my face. Hearing Crash use a big word like agitated lets me know just how pressing this situation is. I gotta drop this fool-ass white boy for sure. I try to think of some hard hip-hop, the toughest rap song going. Young Jeezy, Lil' Wayne and Birdman, somebody like that. Mood music. I need a sound track to help me drop fool-ass white boy Benny.

I look deeper at Benny. His hands are still down at his sides. At least he has the sense to admit he doesn't know what to do with his fists. I've got mine up as if I'm about to get my Floyd Mayweather or Oscar de la Hoya on.

"Eric Posey the Poser," Crash chides.

Poser? He's probably right.

Crash moves toward me, pushes one of his baseball-mitt-sized hands against my shoulder blades. That move edges me forward. His voice has a sharp corner to it as he says, "Kick this white boy's ass or I'm gonna kick yours. You understand?"

I look at Benny apologetically. Hope he understands. He seems as if he does. He raises his hands finally, both of them touching, giving him the appearance of praying. I step forward, some of Young Jeezy's hard thug music ringing in my head, and plant the best right hand I've ever thrown—okay, the only right hand I've ever thrown—deep into Benny's soft gut. Benny folds over immediately. I'm in church with my mother at that moment. "Victory Is Mine," that gospel song, replacing the Jeezy in my head. But then Benny hurtles forward suddenly, catches me seriously off guard, grabs my knees, and pushes me tumbling backward. We wrestle around on the ground. He's slippery, hard to grip, but I get some kind of hold on him. It's not a good hold. And unfortunately he's got one on me, too. I can hear Crash singing that stupid song in the background as I struggle to beat up Benny: *"A fight, a fight, A black and a white. If the black don't win, We all jump in...."*

Crash says, "Aiight, Poser. Chill. Quigley is heading this way."

Benny lets his grip on me go. I do the same with him. Both of us jump up and brush off, doing our best to avoid being dealt the swift hand of discipline from Mr. Quigley, the school's chief hall aide. Detention would mean no surfing the Internet or MySpace for Benny or me, plus the added indignity of a beating from one of my mama's switches, in my case. Neither one of us wants that. I particularly wouldn't want to deal with Mama. Just the thought of her discipline makes me want to cry big crocodile tears.

Benny and I take off in separate directions, spared for the time being.

Crash is beside me, walking calm, with a bop I've practiced in front of my mirror but can't seem to get right. The girls love how Crash moves. They don't love how I move. They don't love how I dress. They don't find me cool unless midterms or finals are coming up. Then I'm the tutor king, overlooking how utterly dumb some of these girls are because they smell good and their Apple Bottoms fit so snug.

Crash's long stride matches my half run.

I ask, hopeful, "I kicked his ass, Crash?"

"If the black don't win, we all jump in," he replies. He shakes his head and looks at me with eyes painted with pity. I'm used to that look.

"He picked Poser up and body-slammed him," Crash announces to the assembly in the locker room. I'm at the eye of the storm, at the center of my peers as they surround me. They all look alike. Timbs, throwback jerseys, bald heads or cornrows. I look like some form of Kanye West or Pharrell: cardigan sweater, khaki pants, suede Wallabees. I still get no play. Kenya's best friend, Lark Edwards, she's summed it up on more than one occasion: "You're trying, Eric, I give you that. I mean, you're really trying." At least she sounds sincere when she says it.

Trying, that's the key word. Close but no cigar. A cliché, I know. I hate clichés, but that one fits me. I'm just missing that element that comes so naturally to most of the other boys. That element that can't be bottled, can't be manufactured. Cool. It gives them confidence. And I'm missing cool in the worst way.

I keep my eyes focused on my suede Wallabees.

I can't look any of the cool boys surrounding me in the eyes.

"He did get in one weak *jab*, though," Crash says on my behalf.

I look up as those words are spoken and wait. Hopeful that my one swing will draw me some kind of reprieve, that I'll get some level of respect from everyone instead of the usual pity or taunts.

"A jab," someone says. "Benny don't weigh but a buck five and all this lame got off was a jab?"

My shoulders slump at ease; these guys will never grant me a reprieve. Never. My gaze falls back on my Wallabees.

Crash says, "You know the deal with this dude. Eric Posey the Poser."

I retrieve my backpack from the bench in front of my locker, prepared to make another of my many tail-between-the-legs exits. I'm almost beyond the circle of cool boys when Crash pulls me back by the shoulder and wrenches the backpack from my hands.

"Give me that. What you got in here you always guarding so hard, Poser?" he says, reaching his hands into my bag and pulling out a black-and-white composition book.

"M-my Book of Rhymes," I say, upset at myself for stuttering and being so slow of hand.

"Book of Rhymes..." Crash studies the book. "My dude, you are straight-up obsessed with those fake rap cats, always talking about some phony rapper. What, you a closet MC now, Poser?"

I reach for the book. Crash holds it above his head and well out of my reach. Even on my tiptoes I fall inches short of getting my hands on it again. I'm a high school sopho-more, just five-seven. Looking for a growth spurt, like someone looking for love with Tila Tequila.

"Let me see what you spittin'," Crash says.

"Give it back, Crash." My voice is barely a whisper. I know it. I hate that about myself.

"'Seen my lady home las' night, Jump back, honey, jump back,'" Crash reads from my book. "'Hel' huh hand an' squeeze it tight, Jump back, honey, Jump back.'" Crash looks up at me, perplexed. "What's this, Poser?"

I hang my head in shame. "Paul Laurence Dunbar... it's poetry."

The others snicker. Wannabe Paul Wall grills blind me. Crash shakes his head and tsks at me. "Thought you said it was rhymes, Poser? Real rhymes."

I say, "Rappers are our modern-day poets. Look at Talib Kweli, Common, Nas—"

Crash puts his hand up to halt me. "I ain't trying to get no Hip-hop 101 lesson, Poser. Aiight? So shut up."

I shut up briefly.

Then a thought gnaws at me and I say, "I'm just point-ing out the correlation between rap and poetry."

Crash looks around the room at everyone, says, "Did this nigga just say 'correlation'?"

One of the others pipes up. Kid in a LeBron James jersey. I couldn't tell you his name. "Poser has a point, Crash." Everyone looks at him, like he's the real LeBron James, a human highlight film replayed over and over on ESPN. He's one of the cool boys. That's how it is with them, they command attention. I want to be one of them so bad it hurts. Hurts like a bad tooth. "Check this," the faux King James says. And the room quiets to hear what he has to offer. I've learned not to be overly hopeful. I'm sure this isn't going where I'd like it to. Still, I wait. Maybe this one time...

"Instead of Tupac Shakur," King James continues, "we can call your boy...Two Packs of Sugar."

They all burst out laughing. Even Crash, who rarely cracks a smile, has one on his face. I bite my lip. Death, taxes and me being picked on—the only certain things in life.

Crash looks at me, says, "Nigga, you disappoint me."

I clear my throat. For once I'm going to fight for my dignity. "A Tribe Called Quest tried to say *nigga* was a term of endearment on the *Midnight Marauders* album...but I don't like the word, Crash. So don't call me that."

Crash places my composition book back in my bag nicely but then hurls the fifteen-pound JanSport backpack at me. I'm not prepared for that hammer throw. The bag plunks against my chest and knocks the wind from me for a second. I almost topple over but somehow keep my balance, stay on my feet. More laughter comes from the others in the locker room. It fills our space like music.

Crash says, "*Nigga,* get on up out of here before there be a *correlation* between my foot and your ass."

I leave without another word or complaint to a chant of "Poser, Poser, Poser."

Mr. Atkins scribbles his indecipherable handwriting across the chalkboard, taps the board with the chalk when he's finished, and turns to face the class. Benny's sitting one row to my left. We haven't spoken a word since our aborted fight. Crash is directly in front of me, sound asleep, snoring lightly. He does this through most of his classes. Even the really difficult ones, like trigonometry, where paying attention is vital. Sleeps them away. Yet, somehow, he always is granted a passing grade. I can't think of many teachers willing to sign off an F on Crash. I shudder to think how little Crash will know when he graduates, how unprepared he will be for the real world. But that's not my boat to row.

Mr. Atkins, however, is one teacher brave enough to give Crash the grade he actually deserves, even if it is a failing one.

Crash had better watch himself.

"Shakespeare wrote sonnets of fourteen lines," Mr. Atkins says from the front of the classroom. "The rhyme scheme is ABAB, CDCD, EFEF, GG...so the first line rhymes with the third, second with the fourth, and the last two lines rhyme with each other."

Mr. Atkins starts a slow stroll down the center aisle. I tap Crash's shoulder to try and jar him, but he shrugs me off and continues his head-back slumber. Atkins reaches Crash's desk and slams his hand down hard on the surface. It echoes like a gunshot. Crash is unmoved. He sleeps through similar sounds every night at home. His projects are beset by the things that turn boys into men way too fast: guns and sex. Gangs and pimps and prostitutes. The intersection of which often ends with gunshots. Mr. Atkins fires a second shot. Crash slowly rises, wipes at his eyes and blinks from the harshness of the overhead track lights. There is no sense of urgency in him.

"Shakespeare's sonnets were written in iambic pentameter," Atkins says. "Would you know what that is, Percival?"

"Each line has ten syllables and every second syllable is stressed," I call out in an attempt to save Crash. He and Mr. Atkins are like fire and ice. Mr. Atkins and Officer Gerard, who mans the metal detector when we enter the building in the morning, are the only adults I can think of brave enough to call Crash by his given name. I give Mr. Atkins *mucho* credit, because Officer Gerard has a gun on his hip.

Mr. Atkins frowns. "I figure you know, Eric. I wanted Percival to get one." He sighs and looks off at some faraway spot. "Just *one* this semester and I'd—I'd buy the entire class pizza." Mr. Atkins smiles and looks at a weary Crash. "I don't think I'm in any danger of having to pay up on that bet, though. Am I, Percival?"

Crash's jaw muscles tense. He balls his hands into fists

but wisely keeps them obscured under his desk. A few brave souls in the back of the class snicker and laugh. I feel bad for Crash. I would shield him from this humiliation if I could. I know what it's like to have laughter directed at you. It isn't a good feeling.

Mr. Atkins says, "Stay awake, Percival. Next time you shut your eyes, I'm shutting you out of this class. I'll remind you this class is a requirement for graduation." Atkins turns on his heels at that and starts walking back toward the front of the room. "Can anyone name a famous poet?"

Crash turns to me, spit flying from his mouth. "Give me a name, Poser. I want to shut this dude up once and for all. He stays on my back. I need to get him up off me."

"What?"

"Give me a name," Crash says, his mouth foaming, spit flying. A drop of indignity lands on my nose. "Name of a poet, you stupid lame."

Stupid lame?

I think back to the teasing session in the locker room, all the times Crash hasn't returned my friendship, all the times he's broken me down instead of building me up. The tide must change. "E. Lynn Harris," I tell him.

"E. Lynn Harris?" Crash asks, making sure.

"Yeah," I say, sealing the deal.

Crash turns back to the front. "Hey yo, Mr. Atkins?"

Atkins wheels around. Surprise is all over his face. I don't believe Crash has ever spoken up in class before. "Yes," Mr. Atkins says, eyeing Crash.

Crash sticks his chest out. I drop my head and close my eyes. "I have a poet for you," Crash announces.

I open my eyes to see how this plays out.

Atkins furrows his brow. "Do you, now? Will wonders never cease? I guess you like pizza. Go ahead, Percival."

"E. Lynn Harris," Crash says.

I can feel my stomach drop.

Atkins smiles. Time ticks by. The smile widens with each passing second. He's pleased. "You enjoy E. Lynn, Percival?"

"Read all of his stuff," Crash says. "Most of it I've read more than once."

I check my crotch to make sure I didn't wet myself.

"Really now, more than once, is that right? Well, I can't say that E. Lynn qualifies as a poet," Atkins says, "but he's a very good writer. I'm surprised to hear that you enjoy his work, Percival."

"Why's that?" Crash says, loaded to bear. "I can read. I ain't stupid."

"Of course not," Atkins agrees. "It's just that E. Lynn Harris writes novels, and his main characters are usually gay black men in relationships. I didn't think that would appeal to a tough guy like you. I guess you're more tolerant and open than I would have ever given you credit for. Wonders never cease."

Those brave souls in the back snicker again. Crash's shoulders heave. I start thinking about my life six feet underground. You don't humiliate Crash and live to tell about it.

"So unfortunately, no pizza," Atkins says, "but nice try.

At least you contributed for once." Atkins then moves to the far corner of the classroom. "Anyone else want to try? A famous poet. And no one better say Zane."

Laughter from the class.

Crash turns to me, his nostrils flare, his teeth looking jagged as a werewolf's, as if they could cut through the toughest of hides. "That's your ass, Poser. After school. I'm fiddin' to mess a nigga up."

My gaze is on Crash's teeth.

I wonder just how tough my hide is.

I can see Crash waiting for me out in front of the school. He has on an Elgin Baylor throwback jersey. Elgin Baylor was a star on those old Los Angeles Lakers teams, the dynasty that included Jerry West and Wilt Chamberlain. He was Michael Jordan before Michael Jordan. The jersey is sleeveless, accentuating Crash's arms. They look like they were chiseled from granite. He resembles Reggie Bush. My arms, in contrast, look like they were slopped together with Play-Doh. As much as I hate to admit it, I strongly resemble Steve Urkel.

Crash paces back and forth like a wild animal on the hunt, pounding his fist into his hand, working himself up for what will be a one-sided fight. I'd rather walk barefoot on hot coals with a weight around my neck than go out there.

I don't see Mr. Quigley or any other hall aide in sight, but plenty of students are lined up on either side of the walkway. Looks like the dance-off on *Soul Train*. Seeing all of the students, I realize this could be my moment. Facing Crash without fear, regardless of the outcome, is bound to gain me respect and maybe some notoriety. I can picture it, can hear their words of admiration. "See the kid with the dent in his forehead? He stood toe-to-toe with Crash." I'd lose some motor skills but gain respect. That's more than a fair trade.

I step outside. The sun is blazing dead on. Crash has his eyes fixed on some commotion within the crowd of students. The commotion quickly dies down. Crash killed it with a simple look, not wanting anything to take away from his fight with me. He has an intimidating gaze, so hard it makes everything else weak. So much for me facing Crash without fear. I squint, pretending I'm looking into the sun when in actuality I'm attempting to ward off tears. I'd rather walk barefoot on the sun with a weight around my neck than go deal with Crash.

Crash sees me, stops pacing, smiles, and beckons for me to come forward with a nod of his head.

I start moving toward him on legs that have turned to water. My heartbeat is in my ears again, same as the day I fought Benny. The bass line to an even louder and more rambunctious song by Timbaland reverberates in my head. This is fitting, because I'm sure Crash will have me hitting high notes like Justin Timberlake once he gets down to business. Or, probably more fitting, Nelly Furtado.

I stop about ten feet short of Crash. It dawns on me that ten feet of separation is not enough. Ten miles wouldn't be enough to keep Crash from getting back at someone who wronged him. I swallow my fear in a gulp.

He says, "Poser."

"Crash," I manage to reply.

"Hate to have to do you like this, my dude. But you pulled my card."

"Violence never solves anything. It's just a nasty cycle, one that affects our people more than others. We can enact a change, right now, you and me. Black-on-black violence, how sad is that, Crash?"

Crash smiles, says, "Nice speech, but we already got a mayor, my dude."

I want to say something tough. *Brace yourself, fool. Raise up, then, homie.* But instead, in a girl-like voice, that Nelly Furtado tone I spoke of, I say, "Please don't do this."

Crash isn't swayed. He says, "Enough talking," and starts taking steps toward me. I swear the sidewalk cracks beneath his feet as he approaches me.

I close my eyes. And pray. I'm a bit rusty. I get *Now I lay me down to sleep...* and then draw a blank.

Crash is within three feet of me. I drown out the snickers from some of the students, the outright laughter from others, the shouts of those calling me a lame and worse. Focus, like Kobe Bryant said he does when he's playing basketball on the road and the opposing fans are trying their best to get under his skin, throw off his game. The heckling has no effect on him. No fan ever blocked his jump shot. I get in the same kind of zone, a Kobe zone, with my eyes still shut tight. The snickers, the laughter, the insults, bounce right off me.

But my zone is interrupted when a distinctive voice calls out, "Stop!" and a hand touches my shoulder. I jump from my skin like some exotic snake.

"Relax, Eric," from the same voice.

I open my eyes. Benny is standing at my right shoulder, his hands balled into fists. He must have learned from the throw-down with me. His hands are up this time. He appears ready for a fight. Most importantly, he's right by my side. Despite my betrayal, we're a united front. Benny is the kind of friend I've always wished Crash was to me.

Crash pauses and looks from me to Benny, shakes his head. He doesn't even bother to smile.

I say, "Crash, let's just let this go before it gets ugly."

I feel more confident with Benny here.

Crash sings, "Ebony and ivory, live together..."

I say, "You sing more than Ja Rule, Crash."

I'm feeling my Wheaties.

Crash isn't fazed. "It's gonna take more than you two lames to slow me."

I look at Benny. His Adam's apple is bobbing in his throat. He manages to smile, leans in to me and whispers, "I got his legs. You go for his body."

I turn to Crash and home in on the number twenty-two of his Elgin Baylor jersey.

Benny takes off in a run, surprising me with that unexpected move, some kind of Indian war chant rising from his lungs. I have no choice, so I take off, too. My mouth is too dry to scream, though. The fear lodged in my throat wouldn't let any sound pass anyway. I push aside that fear and focus on Crash's body. Benny has his legs. I have his body. Simple enough. Success is achieved by preparation.

Maybe we should have prepared more.

Benny dives low.

Even I can see the move will fail.

It's too telegraphed, executed too slowly.

Crash sidesteps Benny with ease. Benny dives into the sidewalk as if it's a pool, lands without a splash. The Indian war drum is silenced, I realize, as Benny rolls over on the sidewalk and rests there like he's testing mattresses at Sleepy's. Benny's groans are louder than the laughter of the students gathered to witness this massacre.

It's just me and Crash, one on one. Again.

I think of the Karate Kid, Rocky, even *Hoosiers*. In the movies, the underdog is apt to beat the favorite. In real life, the underdog wets his pants and gets punched in the face and gut.

I know.

Both happen to me.

I picked today of all days to wear khakis, light tan khakis.

Crash is on me, pummeling me with punches. My arms don't work. My legs don't work. I can't seem to punch back. I can't get my legs to move, can't run for cover. My Kobe focus is gone, because I can hear the laughter, the snickers and the "Damn, Poser pissed his pants" coming from the crowd of students. I ball myself up as best I can, drop to the ground and take my punishment from Crash.

This is rock bottom. So many times in the past I've thought I was at the deepest part of the well. So many times I thought it couldn't get any worse for me. I was wrong. This is finally rock bottom. They will never forget the dark wet stain on my pants. They will never forget I offered no resistance, no fight whatsoever.

Crash's fist bites into my ear, leaves it burning, stinging, enflamed with pain. Down the road, he'll tell me he held back, he didn't hit me with all his might. And I will accept that. I will accept his lopsided friendship. I'm that desperate.

Crash stops suddenly.

I wait a few ticks and then look up at him.

His breathing is heavy, eyes look so haunted.

Crash starts to say something but doesn't. I manage to get to my feet, move over by where Benny is crumpled on the sidewalk. I offer him my hand, help him up. He pats my back. Our friendship is resurrected. I look over to Crash. He is still standing in the same place, still breathing heavily, eyes still haunted.

I don't hate him. Believe it or not, I actually feel sorry for him. Something is missing in his life. Just like something is missing in mine. In that way, if in no other, we are brothers, we are bonded, we are the same. That gives me some comfort.

Crash continues to watch me. He says nothing.

I have so much I'd like to say to him, but I don't say anything, either.

I have wounds to lick. I move away, off to lick them.

The students who witnessed the massacre part like the Red Sea, let me through. Their laughter and mocking words don't even bother me. I'm used to it, even if this is worse than most days. I can handle this. Alone, I know, but that's the breaks.

Rock bottom is a lonely place, for sure.

kenya

I could have literally died.

Like a black person in the first few minutes of a horror picture.

You know they put us to an end before the opening credits have finished. That's cool, though. Get us out of there early in the movie. Let them dumb blond chicks run screaming through the woods just to fall down when Jason or Michael Myers gets close with his ax. Let them dumb blond chicks catch a fair one. That's just fine by me.

Pardon *moi* for that digression.

Anyway, like I said, I could have literally died.

It was the talk of the school. I got so many text messages and phone calls on it I went ahead and turned my cell off. Imagine that. I live for my cell phone. Think about how hard it was to power it off. But I couldn't handle all the chatter. *Kenya's little brother got kicked around like a can* and *peed in his pants.* Just like that I understood the shame Brandy must feel dealing with Ray J's scandals. It wasn't a good feeling. Not the least bit.

And to think, I almost made it out of high school without a blemish. I'd never gotten dissed by a boy. Didn't get my very first period on a day I just happened to wear white capris. And I didn't have to rush to the lunchroom the day after cheerleader tryouts to see if my name was posted. The cheerleading coach, Mrs. Jonas, she'd come to me asking that I be on her team. A personal solicitation.

All told, my high school experience looked better than Boris Kodjoe.

That's until Eric messed it all up for me. Senior year was supposed to be relaxing. I was supposed to coast by. All of that went out the window the moment Eric stupidly insulted Crash. What was my brother thinking? Was he crazy? No one insulted Crash. That was an unspoken rule in our school. You had to have more screws loose than a janitor had keys to willingly get on Crash's bad side.

I said, "My stupid brother. I don't know how we came from the same womb."

"Don't be angry with Eric, Ken. He's going through enough as it is. He needs your support. I feel so bad for him."

Lark Edwards, my best friend. Offering up unwanted advice. What did she know? Toughest thing she'd had to deal with all year was choosing which ringback tone to program on her cell phone. Akon or Young Jeezy? Robin Thicke or Lil' Wayne? I'd told her about Verizon Wireless's Jukebox system—she could pick several songs, and every time someone called her phone, a different, randomly selected ringback tone would play. It switched things up lovely, kept it fresh for anyone trying to reach her. Problem solved. Lark was smart enough to get skipped ahead two grades but couldn't figure that out on her own. Go figure.

I shook aside Lark's well-intentioned advice and said, "Needs my support? He needs Depends. He peed his pants, Lark. Right now I'm feeling like a sex tape with Kim Kardashian wouldn't be so bad."

"Oh, Ken. Don't be so dramatic. Three soldiers died in Iraq today. On the scale of things, this is nothin'."

"And this too shall pass?"

"Right. Exactly. Is anybody still talking about Michael Jackson dangling his baby over the balcony? Or Janet's boob popping out at the Super Bowl? Even serious stuff…9/11, the Virginia Tech shooting. Nope. We're in a culture that is quick to forget."

I did my best to believe her. We were at the mall. The Against All Odds store. Usher and R. Kelly were blasting from the sound system, figuring out between them that they were dating the same girl. I loved Against All Odds because the clothes were tight to death and they always had something hot bumping through the speakers. It was like shopping and a club experience wrapped into one. Can't think of any other store where you can get yourself a cute outfit and a cute dude at the same time. Where trying on clothes meant dancing in front of a mirror. I needed the diversion after what Eric had brought to my doorstep.

I had three hangers with clothes in my arms. A Baby Phat top and bottom. Some Enyce jeans.

"You'll look so right in them BPs, Ken. Love those jeans." Lark crinkled her nose. "Leave the Baby Phat top, though. Not feeling that."

I moved over to a mirror, held the jeans up in front of me. "You ain't ever lied, Lark. These jeans are the truth. But I like the top, too."

"It'll be too tight. You got too much stuff for that shirt. Donnell Tucker is gonna trip if you wear that to school."

I sang like Keyshia Cole and had a chest like her, too.

Donnell'd been sniffing after me since freshman year. I couldn't be bothered. He was lame. Wore Ecko jeans with old-school FUBU sweaters. A word of advice to the fellas: never mix your designers. But that was Donnell. Crazy like that.

"I ain't studying Donnell Tucker, Lark."

"Still holding out for Boris Kodjoe?"

"Am I."

"I don't see it happening, Ken."

"I've got a backup plan. Worse comes to worse I'll make do with—"

"Taye Diggs," Lark finished.

It was one of my frequent lines. She knew me well. We had four years of friendship under our belts. I liked to think we'd always be tight. That we wouldn't drift apart like most did when they left high school for college and the real world. That one day we'd be in the park sharing phone pictures of our kids while they played in sandboxes. I'd be Miss Kenya to her children, and she'd be Miss Lark to mine.

In a singsong voice, Lark said, "Bet you'd be singing a different tune if I said Ricky Williams."

"Ricky's okay. Nothing special. I shop for me, not some dude in school. That's a recipe for disaster, making moves based on how some guy is gonna respond to it. I can't even be bothered." I added a dismissive wave of my hand to solidify my point.

Most of that was a lie.

I had to downplay my true feelings for Ricky, though. Otherwise I'd get burned. Just like Mama. She'd stamped into my head that a woman should never love a man more than he loved her. Or equal, for that matter. Men weren't to be trusted. They were a necessary evil, true, but they weren't to be trusted. Her nasty divorce from my father was exhibit A. The trifling relationship she had with "the boyfriend," as I referred to her current paramour, was exhibit B. I wasn't trying to let Ricky be exhibit C.

I refocused, asked Lark, "What about you? David Rivers has been trying to holla for a minute."

"Negative."

Lark was hard to figure. David Rivers ran point on the varsity basketball team. Six-three in his socks. LL Cool J dimples. Muscular. Built more like Fif than LL, though.

You know, big arms, thick through the middle, whereas LL has a more tapered waistline. David's cocoa-colored skin was smooth all over. Teeth were whiter than Wonder bread. And he had strong hands and big feet. David was the truth.

I said, "I'm gonna start wondering about you soon, Lark."

She looked at me. Hard. "What's that supposed to mean? Wondering what?"

"You ain't going Sheryl Swoopes on me, are you?"

Sheryl Swoopes was a WNBA player. She'd come out of the closet not too long ago. Left her husband to date her female coach. Gave new meaning to the phrase *playing on the same team.*

Lark batted her eyelashes, licked her lips, moved to touch my arm. "Hmm, you figured me out. What's that Fab song…? 'My girlfriend's got a girlfriend,'" She grabbed my wrist, ran her hand up my arm, stopped at my chin, and caressed it with her soft fingers. It all happened so fast I couldn't react quickly enough. "Come here, sexy. Sexy Kenya."

I swatted her away. "Stop playing, Lark."

"Can the two of us fit in dem jeans, mama?"

"If you don't—"

Lark broke out laughing. "Relax your mind, Ken."

"I'm saying…"

"I am looking forward to your next pajama party, though."

"Lark!"

She put her hands up. "Okay, I'll stop."

"You're crazy, girl."

"All day, every day."

The Shop Boyz was partying like rock stars through the store's speakers at that point. I swayed sexily to their rhythms as I continued to look around the store. Lark was busy looking at clothes, too. Why, I didn't know. She hardly ever bought anything. Her folks' money was funnier than Katt Williams, she always said. And yet she always managed to have fly gear. A gift, she'd say every time she showed up with something new. Never did say who her benefactor was, though. And I never asked.

After a while Lark announced, "David just doesn't fit into my life, Ken. That's all."

It'd been a moment since we'd spoken about him. I'd forgotten that conversation.

But I said, "Use it or lose it."

Lark looked at me, wide-eyed. "Use it or lose it. What are you saying? You're using it?"

I didn't answer.

She got right up in my face.

"Ken, please tell me you didn't go and give up the goodies without telling me about it."

I hadn't.

But close.

Real close.

Ricky'd seen me in some boy shorts. Matter of fact, he'd bought them for me. Said he liked how I looked in them. Moaned and licked his lips like he didn't have sense when

I modeled them. "Turn around, Kay. Ooh, turn around again, Kay." At one point I was sneaking him into my room at least three nights a week. Just like in the movies. Except he didn't have to throw a rock at my window to get me to open up. He'd send me a simple text message: LMIK, translation "Let me in, Kay." That's right, we had our own language. Our vibe was incredible. We kissed all the time, something most of these dudes weren't trying to do. We rubbed up against each other so much I'm surprised we didn't catch fire. We didn't do the do, though. I always stopped him right before it reached that point.

Maybe that's why the text messages slowed.

He still hollas on occasion. But not like he used to.

I missed it.

Mama would've said I deserved it if she knew how much I gave of myself to Ricky Williams.

She'd probably be right.

"Kenya?"

"What?"

"You blocking me out?"

"No."

"Answer my question, then."

"What's your question?"

"I only asked about five times. You were seriously zoning me out."

"Ask me one more time."

"Did. You. Give. Up. The. Goodies?"

"No. I. Didn't."

"Pinkie swear, and may you grow Michael Jackson's nose if you're lying."

I tell you, sometimes I thought Lark wanted to be a Jackson. She was always bringing their names up into something. Michael and Janet especially. But she was known to throw La Toya and Jermaine's names around, too. Shoot, I'd even heard her mention Randy a few times. Now, who other than Katherine or Joseph did that?

"Come on, Ken. If that's true, I want you to pinkie swear right now."

I'd promised Ricky that when I was ready, no matter what the circumstances, I'd let him be my first. I wonder if that still applied being as we hardly ever talked anymore. I believed it did.

Lark said, "Pinkie swear, Ken."

I nodded, then hooked my pinkie with hers. I wasn't about to tell her the whole truth about me and Ricky, though. Lark was my girl and all, but her mouth was a sieve. She was the Wendy Williams of our school. Couldn't keep a secret to save her soul. Serious diarrhea of the mouth.

We moved around the store at least ten more minutes without another word between us. I measured time by songs in Against All Odds. Justin Timberlake moaned about his summer love. Ne-Yo wondered aloud if his ex ever thought about him anymore. And Fab, in a cute ghetto way, let his girl know that he and she together equaled better math. Like I said, about ten minutes had passed, all told.

Then, suddenly, Lark said, "Damn, Ken. I. Do. Not. Believe. This. The universe is at play here. Has to be. This can't be a coincidence."

If she was talking about what I thought she was, then she was right, this wasn't a coincidence. I'd heard more rumors than I could stand regarding Ricky. I'd come to the mall for myself to see if they were true. I prayed they weren't. The slander of haters.

"What are you talking about, Lark?" I asked as innocently as possible.

"Guess who just walked in."

I turned to see, already knowing what I'd find.

Ricky Williams.

My heart started to beat. Well, it probably had been beating all along, but seeing Ricky made me aware of it. Made me aware of my sweaty palms and the knocking of my knees, too. It's a shame the kind of effect that boy had over me, that I let him touch me so deeply, so profoundly. A real shame. Mama would have been so disappointed in me.

"He must have felt you talking about him, Lark," I said slowly.

Lark sucked her teeth. "Dang. Oh no he didn't."

Oh yes he did.

She was referring to the girl Ricky had with him. I didn't know her. From a different school, I'd heard. Rumor had it her family had some serious money. That she practically lived at the mall, forever buying things for herself and Ricky. I'd heard she bought him an iPod, loaded it with his favorite songs. Homegirl spared no expense. That's why Ricky was with her, I told myself. I ain't saying he's a gold digger, but he ain't messin' with no broke... Had to be that.

Wasn't looks, that's for sure.

She was a light skin thing with good hair, I gave her that. Other than that, she wasn't hitting on much.

Still, it hurt that the rumors were true.

Lark said, "Don't even sweat her, Ken. You're a ten. A dime. She's a two."

"Pretty much."

In unison we said, "*Too* skinny. *Too* tall. *Too* ugly."

I don't know what hurt more, my head or my heart, but I played along.

"He's a trifling dude, Ken. You're right not to give him the time of day."

I said, "They look like Tom Cruise and Katie Holmes."

"Ciara and Bow Wow."

"How tall you think she is?"

"WNBA tall. Manly-looking, too. Bet she's got some Sheryl Swoopes in her."

"You ain't ever lied."

She was tall, but I was exaggerating more than a little bit. Ricky was taller than her by an inch or so. She had to be about five-ten, though. Model height. I was prettier, but I could see her morphing into Tyra Banks later in life. The ugly duckling turning into a beautiful swan. I guess Ricky could envision that as well.

Ricky stopped short when he saw me, tried to back-track. Miss Wannabe Sheryl Swoopes wouldn't let him. She grabbed his wrist like it was a basketball and moved deeper into the store. Ricky hung his head. I don't know why he was tripping like that. He'd obviously made his choice. So he should live with it.

Omarion was coming through the store speakers at that point. He had an icebox where his heart used to be. I did, too.

Lark yelled out, "Hey, Ricky? Pretty Ricky." She didn't have to yell. They were right up on us. Miss Wannabe Sheryl Swoopes was rummaging through a rack of jeans. I wanted to toss the Baby Phat jeans in my hands at her. *Here,* I'd say, *take everything I have.* I wanted to be anywhere but in Against All Odds at that point. I think Ricky did, too.

He looked up, shamefaced. "Oh, hey, Lark…Kay."

Kay. He had nerve calling me that.

I said, "Who's your tall friend, Ricky?"

The girl turned, looked me up and down several times, frowned in appraisal, said, "Monique Thompson. And you know Ricky how?"

"School."

Her eyes narrowed. She plastered a fake smile on her face. "Your name is Kay? That's a cute name. Like something you'd name your pet. Sit, Kay, sit." She laughed it off, gave me a just-joking smile. If she'd been darker, I'd have smacked the black off of her. As it was, I was two steps away from making sure her yellow wasn't mellow.

Ricky tried to move her away. She stood her ground.

I said, "Actually, my name's Kenya. Kay is something only Ricky calls me."

Ricky groaned. I paid him no mind. *Charge it to the game, player.*

"Kenya." Monique said that like she was spitting out stale food. Then she turned to Ricky and repeated it with emphasis. "Kenya." Her hands found her hips and her head was on a tilt at that point.

Ricky hung his head again and sighed.

I asked, "You two okay? There a problem?" They'd come in like Will and Jada. I wanted them leaving like Whitney and Bobby. Like Britney and Kevin.

Monique couldn't hide her disgust. "Yeah, there's a problem. My boyfriend has your name written like a thousand times on this stupid poster in his room."

Her boyfriend?

I regrouped from that bit of news and asked her, "Beyoncé? Or the complete Destiny's Child poster by his window? Couldn't be that LeBron James poster on his door. I'd figure he'd write *your* name on that, seeing as you're damn near LeBron's height."

She frowned and ignored my insult. "Beyoncé. I see you've been in his room."

Ricky groaned again.

He always told me I reminded him of Beyoncé. Matter of fact, he'd started calling me Kay because Jay-Z called Beyoncé Bey. I'd thought it was cute when Ricky and I were hanging tough. I still did, to tell you the truth. I was being hateful with Monique, but all is fair in love and war. The yellow homegirl and I were definitely getting our Baghdad on.

I said, "I'm so sorry beautiful Beyoncé is taken, Monique. But like I said, you deserve to be up on his wall, too." I looked at Ricky. "Get cracking on that, homeboy. Get your girl's name up on LeBron. Today."

Ricky was knee-deep in it. He couldn't form his mouth to say a word.

I turned my attention back to Monique. "It's only right you're on his wall…you're his girlfriend, after all. His significant other. The B to his A. You and him together equal better math. All that good stuff." I laid it on thick.

Monique rolled her eyes. Did that thing we girls do with our necks when we are seriously upset. Looked at Ricky. Hard. Homegirl was looking at Ricky like PETA protestors outside the courthouse eyed Michael Vick when he arrived in his suit, lawyers in tow. For those of you slow on the uptake…she wasn't happy. I wasn't mad in the least. I didn't want her to be happy.

I looked at Ricky again. Wanted to see how he was going to handle this. He avoided my gaze, focused on Monique, said, "It's not her name, Mo. Well, I mean, it is…but not on the poster. I wasn't writing about her on the poster." He stopped, got his lies together. There were probably enough of them to fill the football field at school. "I told you that had to do with Africa. Kenya is one of Africa's—"

Monique put up her hand. "You are so tired. Save it."

"Monique," he whined. I'd never heard Ricky whine before.

"Take me home, Richard."

I almost laughed. Lark actually did.

Monique glared at me, then at Lark, and stomped off. Ricky looked my way, started to say something, and then caught himself. He sighed and shook his head, gave chase after Monique. I wondered if he'd have chased me like that.

Lark called out, "Nice meeting you, Lil' Mo. And see you in school, *Richard*."

I elbowed her in the side. "Stop that. Don't instigate."

When they were out of the store, Lark said, "Homegirl must be on the Barry Bonds diet."

"She was big."

"I was a second away from calling her out of her name, though, when she dissed you with that pet remark."

I looked at Lark. All five feet of her. She made Lil' Kim look tall. I said, "Stop your lying. No you weren't."

Lark smiled. "Okay. I'm just talking greasy, I admit it. I was *scurred*. Who wouldn't be? Homegirl was Amazon.com, Ken."

"You mean an Amazon."

"See...she scurred me so bad I can't even get my thoughts together." She laughed.

I didn't.

I said, "I wonder what he sees in her."

"Ricky's a health nut...maybe he just needed someone to pick fruit from the top of trees for him."

She was trying her best to make me laugh. Trying to ease the pain. I appreciated that. Despite my denials, she knew Ricky had a spot reserved deep inside of me. But Chris Rock and Chris Tucker and Eddie Murphy and Eddie Griffin and all the comics on *Def Comedy Jam* and *The Bad Boys of Comedy* couldn't ease my pain. Mama was right. Giving a man your heart is like turning over the keys to your life. He'll drive your life into the ground and then lose those keys just as quickly. Men can't handle the responsibility. Women's lives are fragile. Handle with care. Ricky'd tossed me around carelessly, broken me into pieces.

Lark said, "You went for homegirl's neck, though, Ken. You took her head clean off with that LeBron stuff. That was brutal. She tried to play you and you struck her back. Bet she doesn't go there with anyone again. I'm proud of you."

I wasn't proud of me.

End of the day, I'd won the battle, but she'd won the war. She'd left with Ricky sniffing behind her like a dog in heat.

That should've been me. I guess I could stop playing he-loves-me, he-loves-me-not over Ricky.

Lark said, "You okay, Ken?"

I smiled courageously. "Yup. At least all that drama made me forget about Eric."

I was reading *The Interruption of Everything,* a very interesting Terry McMillan novel. No matter how hard I tried, I couldn't keep from crying. In the novel, Marilyn Grimes's marriage was falling apart, and her life was devoid of meaning. She was forty-four, and had kids older than me, yet I related to her in so many ways. Everything had been interrupted in my life at the Against All Odds store. I'd given Ricky way too much power. And he'd used it against me. I closed the book, wiped my eyes with a Kleenex and turned on the radio. Hot 97. Angie Martinez was cutting up one minute, cracking all kinds of jokes. Then, next thing I knew, Tamia was talking about "me." How "me" would love her more than *he* ever knew. Another sad love song.

Oh hells no.

I turned that off quick, fast and in a hurry. I didn't have enough Kleenex to be messing with Tamia.

But the music didn't stop. A beat still pulsed through my room.

Then I realized it wasn't my stereo. It was my cell phone. Rihanna's "Umbrella."

The special ringtone I'd assigned to Ricky.

It'd been ringing all day. I'd been ignoring it all day.

I went ahead and checked it that time.

It wasn't a call. An alert for a text message: LMIK.

I got up off my bed and walked slowly to my window. I peeked out, looked up to the end of the street. Ricky's black Honda Accord was parked at the end, like always, being as he couldn't just park it at the curb in front of our house. Mama didn't play that. She wasn't hearing me and any dude. Even though I was about to be eighteen in a few months. She'd set fire to Ricky's car and make him toast marshmallows over the wreckage before she'd let him take her baby girl.

I looked down. Saw Ricky's dark figure casting a shadow on our lawn. He had the sexiest shadow ever. I swear. But I wouldn't let that sway me too much.

I moved away from the window. Blotted my eyes with another tissue and blew my nose and threw on some lipstick and straightened my shirt and fixed my jeans so they rode my waist and prayed and had a miniature nervous breakdown and quickly ran down my options and just as quickly decided what I had to do. Not what I should do, what I had to do. Then, calmly, I went back to the window, opened it.

I heard "Kay" as soon as I pulled the window up.

"What are you doing here, *Richard?*"

"Don't play me, Kay. Let me up, please."

"No."

"I will scream, Kay. I will have the entire neighborhood out here."

"Go away."

"I can't, Kay. I made that mistake once."

The way he said that sounded so sad, so sincere. It melted me.

I undid the latch on my window, lifted the screen. Ricky bolted from the lawn, started climbing. I moved away from the window, went and made sure my bedroom door was locked. Mama wasn't home, neither was the boy-friend, and Eric never left his room, but I liked to be on the safe side. When I turned around from locking up tight, Ricky was standing in my room. He had on a black wife-beater, baggy jeans, and crisp white K-Swiss sneakers. Diamond studs in each ear, a Jesus piece medallion that hung almost to his waist. He looked good. Ten feet sep-arated us. It felt like ten inches. I hated that he had that effect on me. Hated it.

He smiled, said, "You look good, Kay."

I said, "I'm not tall enough to dunk a basketball like a certain female we both know, but I've got my good qualities."

He smirked.

"How's your tall friend, Richard?"

He shook his head. "Not good."

"That why you're over my way?"

"Not at all. Come on."

"Uh-uh."

"You know me better than that, Kay."

"Do I?"

He nodded, moved toward me. Sean John's Unfor-givable. That's the cologne he was wearing. It fit. What he'd done to me was unforgivable. Truly.

He stopped a foot short of me. "Kay?"

"My name is Kenya, please."

"I can't call you Kay?" His eyebrows arched in surprise.

I shook my head. "You forfeited that right, player."

"Okay…Kenya?"

"That's my name, don't wear it out."

"Why are you being so hard, girl?"

"Are you serious?" I asked.

"Okay, you're right." He put his hands up in surrender. "I understand. I messed up."

I shrugged. "No biggie. Don't even sweat it."

He moved closer, took my hands. I let him. "It was a biggie. I was stupid. I'm talking Michael-Vick-dog-fighting stupid. Britney-Spears-baby-on-her-lap stupid. Foxy-Brown—"

I cut him off with "You love her?"

He shrank by several inches. "Monique? Are you kidding me? I just turned eighteen. Love doesn't live here."

I snatched my hands away. He'd told me he loved me at one point.

"Kay."

"Kenya," I said.

"Real talk?"

"Whatever, Richard."

"Can you stop that? Ricky, please."

"Whatever, Ricky."

He plopped down on my bed. I didn't like that. I hadn't offered him that spot. He patted a place next to him, wanting me to sit down beside him. He must've fallen on his head on the climb up. I shook my head. His eyes were cast down, sad. I looked away. If I didn't, in a minute I'd be sitting on his lap, playing with his ears or something.

He said, "Okay, real talk... Monique was just something to do. A way to pass the time."

I wheeled back around, angry, said, "Johnny Cochran you are not. So you like using girls just to pass the time?"

He surprised me, said, "Pretty much."

Oh hells no. I moved over to my window, pointed at it. "Leave, Richard."

"Hear me out?"

"I've heard enough."

He said, "'Girlfriend.'"

"What?"

"That Alicia Keys song," he said. "You had her CD playing that night you modeled those boy shorts for me."

"So?"

"I brought over Italian hot dogs for us. You let me eat the fries off your dog."

I didn't say anything.

He continued, "You didn't have on any perfume, but you'd showered before I came over. You smelled like Dove. Dove never smelled so good."

I still didn't say anything.

"You'd been reading that Toni Morrison novel *Song of Solomon*. I asked you why you were always reading. You shrugged. I picked it up, read a bit of it. It was pretty good. 'Milkman lay quietly in the sunlight, his mind a blank, his lungs craving smoke. Gradually his fear of and eagerness for death returned.' You remember that passage, Kay?"

I nodded. I couldn't believe he remembered. He didn't seem that enthused at the time, as I recall.

He said, "I do, too. In fact, I remember that and everything else about that night."

I gulped, asked, "Why?"

He paused and then said, "Because you weren't just something to do, a way to pass time. I got twisted up in this thing, fo' sho'. Did some things I regret. I wanna make it right with you. If you'll let me."

"Why should I? Just words. Anybody could say what you're saying."

Big talk that I didn't even mean, but I couldn't just give easy.

He nodded. "If you'll allow me to spend some time with you again…my actions will speak louder than my words."

"Been there, done that."

"Let's go back," he begged. "One-mo-again."

I thought about everything.

He remembered the song I'd been playing that night.

How I smelled.

Toni Morrison. I repeat, Toni Morrison.

He said, "Pretty please, Kay."

I didn't correct him about my name. I said, "Begging really suits you well, Richard."

He sighed. Long and hard. Then he said, "I'll do anything, Kay. For just one more chance with you."

"Admit on your MySpace page that you really really

really like Kelly Clarkson. Let 'em know you find your-self singing 'Since You've Been Gone' in the shower."

"Damn, Kay, since when you got so mean?" He smiled at that. He knew he was close to breaking my resolve. If I was making light of our situation, things were moving in his favor. I couldn't stand him for reading me so well.

I said, "You really hurt me, Ricky."

He said, "Hurt myself, too, Kay. Bad."

I silently apologized to my mama, went over to Ricky.

"Hold me, Richard Williams."

"Ricky," he said as he took me in his arms.

"And I'm Kay," I said to the shoulder I lay my head against.

"I hope you know what you're doing."

"I don't."

"He actually remembered all that?"

"Yes, Lark."

She whistled through the phone line. "Who'dathunkit?"

I said, "I actually have a boyfriend."

"And you're sure Ms. Amazon.com is out of the picture?"

"S'what he says."

"I'd be scared."

"You think I'm not?"

"I can imagine. And he actually remembered the Toni Morrison passage?"

"Yes, Lark."

"That's deep. Toni Morrison's deep. I bet you *she*

doesn't even remember the passage. And she wrote the darn thing. I'm thinking Oprah and Ricky are the only two people on the planet who'd remember that passage."

I smiled at that. Lark had a point. That one move showed me how much Ricky really cared.

"You gonna tell your momma about him, Ken?"

"Is you crazy?"

"She'd understand. Ain't things going well with her new boyfriend?"

I didn't answer that.

I didn't like to think about my mother's boyfriend.

In any way.

Mama had been set up with the boyfriend by a meddling, self-proclaimed matchmaker extraordinaire coworker. Woman knew of him through her sister's cousin's boyfriend's uncle. A long and disastrous chain of liars. I'll never forget the night Mama was preparing for her first real date with "the boyfriend." They'd talked on the phone for at least a couple weeks, felt ready to take things to the next level. Mama modeled five outfits for me, made me pick out the winner among the bunch. If I'd known then what I know now, I wouldn't have crinkled my nose at the doo-doo brown outdated dress she'd put on first; I'd have given it an enthusiastic thumbs-up. Mama talked and talked the whole time it took her to get ready. Nerves, I guess. I remember asking Mama what he looked like.

"Don't be superficial," she'd said.

"Okay, Mama," I replied. "If he looks like the devil on *Hell Date...*"

Mama said, "The who on what?"

"The devil on *Hell Date,*" I informed her. "It's a show on BET."

"Informative and uplifting programming, I'm sure," Mama said, "from the same folks that bring you such fare as *106 & Park.*"

No wonder Eric and I talked the way we did. Mama's name could have been Merriam-Webster. She was a regular old walking dictionary sometimes.

I said, "Yeah. So what he look like?"

Mama beamed. "Five-ten. Athletic and trim. Doesn't smoke or drink. And that's a relief after dealing with your father and his Marlboro Lights...."

I had to laugh.

The boyfriend turned out to be about five feet eight inches with his sneakers on, more than a few pounds removed from any "athletic and trim" physique, if he ever had one, and not a day passed where he didn't have a Heineken in his hand. Oh, on the good side of things, he wouldn't be caught dead smoking a Marlboro Light. Nope.

He preferred Newport shorts.

I needed to stop.

Like they say, if you don't have anything good to say about someone, don't say a word.

Lark interrupted my thoughts with, "Zoning me out again, Ken."

"What happened now?"

Lark said, "Your momma has finally found herself someone special, Ken. She'd probably be able to give you some good advice on the situation with Ricky."

"I doubt it," I said. "Current boyfriend aside, it's always been the same with my mother and her advice about men, especially when it comes to my dad. Don't trust them. Don't believe a word they say. If one even writes you a love letter check it for ricin first."

"Raisins?"

"Ricin, the poison they put on those letters they sent to the senators. We just went over that last week in poli sci."

"I was zoning out on that part, girl."

"Too busy mooning over David Rivers."

"Ken, please. I told you I'm not thinking about that boy."

"I don't want to be the only one with a boyfriend, Lark."

"Do you. It's okay."

"It makes me feel…awkward."

"Look," she said, "you're two years older than me. I got skipped ahead, and we're cool, on the same wavelength with so much, but I'm just not ready for a boyfriend. I've got enough going on to worry about…."

Lark was so smart and so mature, I oftentimes forgot she was the same age as my brother. I guess she was right. Boyfriends could come later.

I said, "I'll leave you alone about David Rivers. Or anybody else, for that matter. I know I'm always on you."

"It's cool. You're looking out. You don't want me to be lonely."

"Never that," I said. "As long as we're friends, you'll never be lonely. I already told Ricky that you and me were gonna continue to hang tough."

"You say that now."

"Lark!"

"I'm joking. I know you have my back, Ken."

I said, "Always. Matter of fact, this Friday why don't we—"

"Gotta go, Ken. Later."

"Lark? Lark?"

Dial tone greeted me.

That happened often when I was talking with Lark. We'd be having the greatest conversation, and then boom, she'd rush off the phone. When I asked her about it later, she always said the same thing: "My parental units came home. They're always on me about being on the phone."

I understood. Mama was tough on me, too.

But I quickly forgot about Lark's issues with her parental units, as she called them. I focused on the larger issue at hand.

I actually had a boyfriend.

Kenya *Williams*. I liked the sound of that; it had a nice ring to it.

Eric

"**BOO** ya! Holla at ya, boy!"

Benny looks over at me with his ocean-blue eyes, smiles, and then quickly turns his attention back to the television set in front of us. It's a state-of-the-art television. Forty-six-inch Sony high-definition set, with a twelve-hundred-watt theater system. Some buttered popcorn and a roomful of black folks talking over the sounds on-screen and we would be at our local Loews movie theater. NBA players run up and down a basketball court in front of us, courtesy of Benny's Xbox 360. Their likeness to the real players is uncanny. The computer-generated images, or CGI, as Benny the Geek is quick to point out, even move with the same fluidity of the real players, with the same cool that a million-dollar contract and an equal number of adoring fans can add to one's self-confidence. Benny uses the Los Angeles Lakers, takes most if not all of his shots with Kobe Bryant. It's the start of the fourth quarter of our game and Kobe already has forty-six points. I run with the Miami Heat, most of my points scored by Dwayne Wade. I'm beating Benny by three points, but the momentum is definitely in his favor. He's on a thirteen-to-two run, has almost completely wiped out my lead.

"Boo ya! Can't stop, won't stop."

Kobe Bryant yet again.

I say, "Would you stop that."

"It's called competition," Benny replies. "It's up to you to stop me, Eric. I won't just lay down for you. But I feel your pain, homie. Kobe is on fire."

"Not that…all that *boo ya* stuff, the hip-hop talk."

"That's how I talk, Eric. *Nahmean?*"

"'*Nahmean'?*" I frown at Benny's word choice. "No, I don't know what you mean. And that's not how you talk. I don't know if I'm playing you or Eminem."

"I'm offended you picked a white rapper, Eric. That's reverse racism. But I'll let you slide on that, homie."

"You're out of control, Benny. I wish you'd stop. That's not how you talk."

"Is now," Benny says, talking to me without looking in my direction, his focus trained on the action on the screen. I talk to him in the same way. If either one of us takes our eyes off the TV, the other gains an advantage. We don't want that to happen. This is serious business. Bragging rights are at stake.

I ask, "Since when have you talked that way?"

"Since Crash did me dirty. Since I became the school's biggest joke—no offense—next to you. I've got two more years there. I'm going to do my best to make them good ones. Can't beat 'em...join 'em. That's my new motto."

I say, "And you think talking like a rapper is gonna get you points?"

Benny says, "Can't hurt to try. I can't go in there talking like Shakespeare." He pauses, forces some kind of English accent. "Thou doth protest my good intentions too fervently. See how ridiculous *that* is, Eric? If it comes down to the Bard or Fiddy, I have to roll with Fiddy."

I want to present the opposing point of view, remind Benny that his "back that thing up" comment to Kenya really started this thing. Remind him that Crash and the others have never taken kindly to some pale white boy speaking in a way that they themselves speak, that they find it insulting and demeaning, that it will cause him more problems than he has now. I say, "I think you're asking for trouble, Benny."

"You're not exactly an expert on the matter, Eric. No offense. But maybe you would find yourself in a better place if you had a little more Fiddy in you than Steve Urkel."

"Steve Urkel?"

"Did I do that?" Benny says in Urkel's whiny voice. "Didn't mean to speak so openly, Eric. But yeah, that's how everyone sees you. I'm sorry."

Steve Urkel.

I've been going for Kanye West, Pharrell, even Common, and somehow I keep ending up like Urkel, arguably the biggest example of a black nerd that exists, the pop culture icon for everything an impressionable black adolescent doesn't want to be.

Lucky me.

Angry, I say, "Well, Benny, I hate to tell you, but they see you in the same light, or worse, because of your lack of melanin. And changing how you speak isn't gonna change that. Just gives them another name to add to geek, nerd, lame, and pizza face: wigger."

Nasty words, I know. I want to hurt Benny in the same way his words hurt me. What he said about everyone seeing me as Steve Urkel is the truth. And, well, the truth hurts. I won't be alone with my pain, though. Benny's gonna share in it.

Benny pauses his Xbox onslaught and looks over at me. I expect some angry words in exchange. That we'll be fist fighting again for the second time in less than a week. I'm prepared for it. Benny says, "Don't hate...congratulate," and goes right back to the game.

It's hopeless.

"You're ridiculous, Benny."

"Word to your mother."

"That's old, Benny. Real old. What you been doing, renting old Spike Lee movies? *Doin' the Right Thing?*"

Benny corrects me. *"Do... Do the Right Thing."*

I say, "I'll pray for you."

Benny says, "Please do. Ask God if there's a place in heaven for a G."

"Ridiculous."

"Boo ya!" Benny shouts, and then adds, "I'm ridiculous. And you are now on the short end of the score. I'll take ridiculous to loser any day, homie."

Kobe again, giving Benny a lead of two points.

I need to focus on the game. I can save Benny's soul after the final buzzer sounds. Maybe. He just might be too far gone.

I grit my teeth, thumb a button on my controller and pass inside to Wade. He's a sure thing. His dunk rattles the rim, ties the score. I tell Benny, "You can't stop him. You can only hope to contain him."

"Eric, Eric, Eric." Benny moves to Kobe again, of course, and shoots a three-point shot from far beyond the arc. The net on the rim ripples as Kobe buries the shot. Benny's now in the lead by three points. One and a half minutes left in the game.

"Lucky shot, Benny."

I attempt a long pass. Bad move. Lamar Odom swoops in and intercepts the pass, dishes the ball immediately to Kobe, who shoots another three. Dead-on, nothing but net. I'm down six in the blink of an eye.

Benny says, "This is why I'm hot. That pass is why you're not," and laughs at his little rhyme.

I don't reply to that. But if he starts saying *ay-bay-bay,* we will definitely find ourselves in a fistfight. There are certain lines that just can't be crossed.

Dwayne Wade cuts into Benny's six-point cushion. I'm down four with a minute to go.

Kobe misses.

Dwayne Wade doesn't.

I'm down two points with forty-five seconds.

Benny says, "Okay, you're doing a lil' somethin' somethin'. But I'm not shook."

Kobe clanks another shot. He picked the perfect time to go ice-cold. God bless his CGI heart.

I grab the rebound and go inside to old reliable again. Wade ties the score with an easy basket.

The breakdown: Twenty-two seconds left in the game, tied score, Benny's ball.

Kobe dribbles away the clock. I attempt a steal. My bid is unsuccessful.

Six seconds.

Five.

Four.

Three.

Benny finally makes his move with Kobe, darting to the left, then quickly back to his right. My defender is no match for that slick move. Kobe is alone as he elevates for the last shot. He releases it smoothly. The ball moves in slow motion. I sit silent, watch, wait. The buzzer sounds, loud because of Benny's state-of-the-art television. Kobe's shot rattles through the hoop. The CGI Kobe pumps his fist and does a little dance. Benny drops his controller on the plush carpet and throws his hands in the air. Same pose Jay-Z struck at his retirement concert at Madison Square Garden. A winner's pose.

"Dang," I say, disgusted. "I can't believe I blew that lead." My controller also finds Benny's carpet as I throw it down.

Benny moves over to me and rubs my shoulder apologetically.

"Luck," I tell him.

"Don't hate the player. Hate the game," he responds.

All the attempts at cool talk aside, Benny is without question just a geek. His room proves it. It's neat and orderly. There are no posters of swimsuit models on his walls. No Heidi Klum, no Tyra Banks, not even a worn-out poster of Britney Spears. No rap CDs scattered on his desk, even though he's taken the vernacular and attempted to make it his own. I'm not even sure Benny likes music of any kind. I've never seen him listening to the radio, never witnessed him purchase a CD, and MTV and VH1 get no play on his television.

More important than what you won't find in Benny's room is what you will. *GamePro* and *EGM (Electronic Gaming Monthly)* magazines, the jewel cases to any number of video games, comic books and controllers for every video game system invented. If you turn his television on, you're likely to find it on one of two channels: Discovery or G4, the gaming channel.

And then there is Benny himself. He's the best evidence to prove my point.

The things he finds really cool, the things that bring his blood to a steady boil, are things that none of the cool kids at school would find the least bit interesting. I sit in Benny's leather swivel chair at his desk, across the room from him, and watch him in action. He's got this look on his face I can't quite describe. In one class we talked about the "glow" that permeates a woman's skin once she becomes pregnant. Something about hormonal changes that affect the skin. That's it, that's Benny's look.

I call out to him, "Who knocked you up, Benny? Was it Anne Hathaway?"

Anne's a couple shades paler than Benny, with just as much acne, mousy-looking hair and, believe it or not, a pound or two more baby fat than even Benny. She dresses like a movie star—unfortunately, a star from the fifties—Katharine Hepburn or somebody, women old enough for my mother to have to stretch her brain to remember their movies.

All of that, and Benny gets tongue-tied around Anne Hathaway. I don't think he's ever gotten out a word in her presence. I don't even know if she knows Benny exists. It's bad when even the unpopular girls don't know your name.

I say, "Or was it 'Big Bertha' Beatrice?" Nickname says it all.

Benny puts a finger up to his lips, shushes me. He has a cordless phone pressed to his ear; anticipation dances across his pale, acne-scarred face.

I start to say something else, but Benny clears his throat and turns his back to me. "Yes, my name's Mike Hunt," he begins. His shoulders rock as he stifles laughter. "I'm trying to locate a good friend. He had this number last, from what I'm told. I hope I have the right number."

Benny turns to me, smiles wide, mouths *Mike Hunt* and gets a he-he-he look on his face.

Mike Hunt.

Mike Hunt.

Say it slow…*Mike Hunt*. My cu—you get the point.

"Yes," Benny says into the phone. "I've been running into dead ends like you wouldn't believe." He nods and smiles, very proper, not an ounce of wannabe rapper left in the lilt of his voice. "I sure hope so. What's his name?" He pauses for effect. "Ben Dover."

He-he-he.

The person on the other end must think Benny's crazy.

Benny repeats, "Ben. Dover."

I shake my head at Benny's immaturity.

He covers his mouth with his free hand to stifle more laughter, and, unsuccessful, just hangs up the phone. He tosses the cordless to me. I put it on his desk with all the gaming magazines. Benny falls on his bed. He kicks his feet in excitement. "My adrenaline is off the hook, Eric. What a rush."

I say, "You've got problems, Benny."

He says, "I had that lady's mind in the Matrix, Eric. She didn't know which way was up, whether I was feeding her the blue pill or the red pill."

I don't know what he's talking about. He's a real problem when he starts to babble.

He continues. "Wish I'd taped that one, Eric. I'd love to hear it on playback. It was classic."

I say, "That's illegal, Benny. A Homeland Security violation or something."

"I'm not Barack Obama. I'm not on the gubment's list."

I say, "You mean Osama bin Laden."

Benny says, "Same difference."

"Keep joking around about this stuff and get the Feds breathing down your neck."

Benny says, "I'm not scared of po-po."

"Benny, you're scared of Miss Mitchell." Miss Mitchell has mashed-potatoes duty in the school cafeteria. She's known to bark at students in her deep Newport voice if they try to pass her station without getting a healthy spoonful of potatoes. The mashed potatoes are close to inedible, but there isn't a student in our school outside of Crash who'll pass by Miss Mitchell's station empty-handed.

Benny says, "You ever seen that pocketbook Miss Mitchell carries?"

"Have to be Stevie Wonder to miss it," I reply. "It's the size of a suitcase."

"Exactly," Benny says.

"And?"

"I'm not scared of her, Eric. Just cautious. She could easily have a gat tucked away in that thing."

I laugh at the visual of Miss Mitchell pulling a gun from her pocketbook.

Benny says, "You feel me, homie?"

I just nod. What else can I do?

"Homie," I reply. "You're really taking this serious, Benny. You actually think you can remake yourself into one of the cool boys."

Benny looks at me. "Who controls the past controls the future," he says. "Who controls the present controls the past."

"Who is that?"

"George Orwell."

"And not one of the cool boys could tell you who George Orwell is," I remind him.

Benny shrugs. "I don't plan on reciting Orwell in school." He taps the side of his head with a finger. "I'll keep that kind of stuff up here, where it belongs."

"That would be wise."

He says, "In the meantime—"

A loud crash comes from outside in the hall, interrupts Benny before he can finish his statement. Benny frowns, looks at me with concern, and then heads out of his room to investigate. I follow on his heels. I prepare myself to make a run for the door if it is anything remotely dangerous. Mama ain't raise no fool.

"I'm looking forward to you dying, old woman. You are a miserable, miserable woman."

The voice is deep and resentful. It belongs to Benny's father. His father is in the room at the very end of the hall. I know that Benny's grandmother occupies that room. I've never been inside it. The door is always closed. I only know she's in there because Benny gets a hitch in his step every time he passes the door. He talks of her in hushed tones, and with a blatant lack of love. I've always wondered why.

Benny stops at the threshold of the room. I stand right behind him, peering over his shoulder.

"Should just let you rot in this," Benny's father continues. "Save myself from your abuse."

I see Benny's father drop a dirty rag in a brown paper bag next to the bed and crinkle up his nose as he pulls off a pair of white latex gloves. Benny's grandmother clutches her bed rail with arthritic hands. Her fingernails are long, hard and crusted yellow. Fingers so gnarled by arthritis it appears as if she has two hands' worth of fingers on each hand. Her skin has an unhealthy gray-yellow coloring to it. Her full head of white hair is tinted with a sort of dirty green-yellow. White lady composed of more colors than a rainbow.

The room smells like an overflowing trash can in the dead heat of late July.

"I'm not feeding you lunch today," Benny's father announces. "I don't want you having anything else in your stomach. Some ginger ale, that's it."

I can't believe how mean he is to the old woman. Mama's always said that white people are touched by the devil. Just look at how they treat their own parents when their parents become old and helpless. Devils, that's exactly what those white people are.

I've always avoided blanket hate of white folks. Benny's been one of my best friends since the day I met him. Our school is diverse enough that you're going to encounter folks of another race. However, most of the cool black kids stick together in a cocoon. I've never done that. I've never felt bad about venturing out and becoming friends with kids like Benny, either. In truth, the black kids have treated me worse than any white kid ever did.

But now, watching Benny's dad, I'm starting to feel somewhat different.

"Any of that tuna fish left?" Benny's grandmother asks.

Benny's father replies, "I know you're practically blind, but are you deaf, too, you old bag of bones? I said you aren't getting anything."

She snaps back, "I see. I see just fine. And my ears work plenty well, too."

"Wish your mouth didn't work. Shut your trap."

I turn to move away.

Then I hear the old woman's voice calling.

It sounds like she's calling for me.

I turn back to see. Benny presses his hand in my chest, tries to move me back in the direction I was going. I push him aside, move back to the doorway of his grandmother's room. I find a comfortable place in the space and stand there.

"Boy," she says.

"Yes?"

"You see how I'm being treated?"

"Yes."

"Shameful, isn't it?"

I don't reply. It is shameful, but I'm a guest in Benny's home. It's not my place to point out his family's dysfunction.

"Bet your mammy raised you to treat old folks with respect, didn't she?"

I nod. "Yes, Mrs. Sedgwick. She sure did." I take it she meant *mom* when she said *mammy*.

"I could use her," she says. "I can't really blame my son here."

"Quiet with your foolishness," Benny's father says to her.

She swats him away with one of those arthritic hands. "I'm trying to help you. This boy could be the answer to your problem."

I say, "What can I do for you, Mrs. Sedgwick?"

Benny pulls at my shirt. I turn and give him an evil eye. *Let me handle this,* my expression says. In Benny's eyes I recognize certain desperation. I ignore it and shoo him away just like his grandmother shooed away his father.

Benny's grandmother asks, "Your mammy isn't carrying a bundle at the moment, is she?"

I turn back to her again. "Pregnant, you mean?"

"Yes, boy," she says, "pregnant."

"No. Why?"

"Just wondering, boy. I know your women are most of the time."

"Mother..." That's Benny's father again.

Benny continues to tug at my shirt. He can't move me.

Benny's grandmother says, "Your mother raising all those kids on her own. I do have empathy, believe me."

I frown. What does she know about my mother? *All of what kids?* I want to ask. There's only Kenya and myself. What is wrong with this old lady?

She continues, "I know it must be hard. And welfare only takes care of so much."

"Welfare?"

She nods. "That food stamp program is shameful. Are you eating well enough? You look a bit peaked. Scrawny, actually, if I put aside pretense."

I don't know what to say.

She says, "I'm prepared to offer your mammy a job, boy. Wiping an old woman's white ass isn't a duty for her son."

I say, "Mrs. Sedgwick, my mother already has a job. And we're not on welfare."

It's like she doesn't even hear me.

"No," she says, "wiping a white ass is a job for a Negro woman."

My dumbfounded "Say what?" is drowned out by the "Why, Mother? Why?" cry of Benny's father.

Benny pulls at my shirt more forcefully. I finally relent and let him remove me from his grandmother's room. I should have left while the leaving was good, as my mother would say.

"I'm so sorry about that," Benny says.

I look at him through narrow eyes. My heartbeat is very pronounced, pounding my chest like a fist. This is apt, because I feel as if I've been punched. Sucker punched. "You're sorry," I say to Benny.

Benny nods. "Very. She's a sick old woman. Her head isn't right."

For the first time I understand why the black kids don't befriend kids like Benny. We are from two different worlds. We'll never, no matter how much we pretend we could, ever fully understand one another. Martin Luther King was always hopeful that blacks and whites could find common ground, a level of appreciation for one another. Malcolm X was a realist. He didn't like the prospects of that notion. Before today I'd have leaned toward Martin Luther King's belief. But today changes everything. "Separate but equal" works just fine for me.

Benny says, "Let's go play another game of—"

"Nah, Benny. I'm out."

I start moving toward his steps. I notice for the first time how large his house is. The stairway winds and turns and appears to go on forever. The banisters are ornately carved out of wood. The carpeting on the stairs is a rich burgundy. His home is like Tara, the estate from *Gone With the Wind*.

I wonder where the slave quarters are.

"I thought you were staying the night, Eric."

"Changed my mind," I call to him as I start descending the stairs.

"If it's about my grandmother, again, I'm sorry."

"Don't apologize for her. She said what she felt."

"And what are you feeling, Eric?"

I stop at the bottom of the stairs and look up at him. The concern in his eyes is clear. I ignore it.

"Feeling like I made a big mistake."

"What mistake, Eric?"

"Thinking I could be friends with a fool-ass white boy."

"What?" The hurt in his voice is a sound I won't soon forget. But that doesn't matter. Some things have to happen. This moment was preordained. It had to happen.

"Later," I say, and then add, "homie."

"Eric."

I shut the door on his voice.

Shut the door on our friendship, for good this time.

I have a seventeen-block walk ahead of me. Luckily I have my soft Nikes on today. Otherwise I'd be an unhappy camper. The hub station for Metro Transit is on Jeremiah Avenue, far removed from Benny's suburban landscape. I can catch a bus from there back to my hood. I don't know why I ever thought Benny and I could remain as thick as thieves. We're from two different worlds. His street address is 1154 Sycamore Avenue. His street is named after a tree. My street address is 90A Anestio Perdina Boulevard. My street is named after a seven-year-old Mexican boy felled by three stray bullets as he played with his Big Wheel out in front of his parents' duplex. At the end of my block some folks in the community carved a little five-foot-by-five-foot square of empty land into a garden in Anestio's memory. The flowers are kept fresh almost year-round. A cross is staked in the hardest area of ground. A picture of a smiling Anestio is kept secure in a large frame the entire neighborhood chipped in to buy. It's a sad situation that folks have tried to turn positive. Making lemonade out of lemons is how the older folks describe this sort of thing. Where I'm from, that's what you do.

I wipe my brow, frown at the sun, and keep moving at a steady pace. In Benny's neighborhood there are no lemons; everything is naturally lemonade. Homes are well kept and adorned with manicured lawns, cobblestone circular drive-ways, wrought-iron gates, garden gnomes. Lemonade, fruit punch and Kool-Aid, take your pick. No lemons.

No activity on the street, either.

I'm the only soul walking.

Passing by homes with Lexuses and BMWs parked in their garages.

At times like this I wish I had an iPod to listen to. Mama was going to buy me one last Christmas, but I balked at the last minute, asked her for a portable DVD player instead. It wasn't that I didn't want the iPod. I didn't want Mama to spend her hard-earned money pur-chasing one. Times are lean. She's raising Kenya and me by herself for the most part. I hate watching her stretch her finances to provide for us. Hate the sacrifices she makes to ensure that Kenya and I don't go without. Mama wears shoes until the heels fall off. She seldom buys new clothes. She gets all of her toiletries and beauty items at the Dollar Tree. It's a tough way of living.

So I told her I didn't want an iPod after all, that a portable DVD player would suit me just fine. It wasn't a lie. I enjoy movies almost as much as music.

Of course, by the time she finished buying DVDs for my portable player she could have gotten me two iPods. I woke up Christmas morning to two large wrapped presents. One box was the DVD player. The other box was the DVDs. All of my favorite actors and actresses were represented: Eddie Murphy in *Boomerang;* Denzel in *Out of Time* and *Training Day;* Mekhi Phifer in *Paid in Full;* Jamie Foxx in *Collateral;* Ray Liotta in *Smoking Aces.* There were many more, too many to list.

I've got the best mama.

Six blocks to go.

I wonder what Benny's up to. Whether he went straight back to playing with his Xbox after I left. Whether he's having a heart-to-heart with his father about the hatefulness of his grandmother. Whether they're conversing about an idealistic world where people are judged by the content of their character and not the color of their skin.

Benny's been a good friend, I must admit.

But other friends will come.

At least, I hope so.

Finally, the bus station is in sight. The walk over wasn't so bad after all. The blocks are short, nothing like what you'd find in the city. I can see the kiosk where riders wait to be picked up. Nothing like it exists in Benny's neighborhood.

The kiosk's glass is frosted from wear and tear. There's a schedule posted in flimsy plastic casing attached to the glass. I'm alone at the station. I run my finger over the schedule, find my bus's arrival time.

I have another twenty minutes to kill.

I have a seat on the bench in the bus kiosk.

Wait. Alone, as usual.

Here comes the bus, finally.

Twenty minutes late.

I stand up, fish in my pocket for coins and move to the curb. The door opens and I step up. The driver is a portly middle-aged black man with a patchy growth of hair on his chin. Hair also grows out of his ears. I look at his left hand as I drop my coins in the slot. No wedding ring. I notice that his gray uniform shirt carries remnants of his lunch. Ketchup and mustard stains. My biggest fear is that I will end up just like him in thirty years. That I'll be hearing chants of *"Poser, Poser, Poser"* for the rest of my natural life.

The bus is crowded; the only available seats are way in the back. I move toward one, which is directly across from two girls I've seen before at school. I don't know their names. They're in the popular crowd. Kenya knows them, though, I'm sure. One is busy bopping her head to the music coming out of her iPod. The other is busy watching me move down the aisle, chewing her gum like it's going out of style. Ms. Bazooka elbows the other girl in the side and nods her head in my direction as I approach.

I pretend I don't see them as I drop into a seat directly across the aisle from where they sit. Again I wish I had an iPod I could get lost in. Wish I had brought my Nintendo Game Boy along with me. Even my portable DVD player would be okay. I could plug in my earphones and absorb one of my movies. But I don't have any diversion. As usual, it's just me.

My stomach churns with nerves. My hands are sweaty. My mouth is dry. My heart is a drum in my chest. I expect some drama in one, two, three...

"You go to Marcus Garvey, don't you?"

I keep my posture and head straight ahead.

I did not hear Ms. Bazooka address me.

"Hey," she half yells between hard chews on her gum.

I can't hide. I turn in her direction. "Hey," I say, mimicking how I've heard Crash speak to girls. "What's cracking?"

Ms. Bazooka's nose wrinkles. "*'What's cracking?'* That's pretty lame."

I try again. "What's good?"

She says, "Too late," and iPod giggles. She's turned her music off. Not a good sign. I'm about to get double-teamed, for certain. This is exactly why I've been hesitant to venture outside my home since what I refer to simply as the Incident.

Ms. Bazooka says, "You're Kenya's brother."

It isn't a question. I nod in answer, though.

iPod says, "That's gotta suck...for Kenya."

Okay, this is about to get really bad. My only remaining hope is that they didn't see my fight with Crash. That they're unaware of the specifics of that situation. That, even though they attend the same high school as me, and talk of the fight is pretty much dominating everyone's mind, they're not aware of just how badly my fisticuffs with Crash turned out. That they don't have MySpace pages and haven't visited any of the more than two dozen pages that reference my fight with Crash.

Ms. Bazooka says, "Kenya's gonna be fine. Eric here, too, I see. He's not wearing a neck brace. That's a good sign." She slaps hands with iPod. iPod giggles. I hate her giggle.

So much for hope.

Everyone knows. Girls who never noticed me, and certainly didn't know my name, now do.

I'm the laughingstock of the entire school.

I say, "Crash is one of my best friends, ladies. I was uncomfortable fighting him."

Ms. Bazooka says, "With friends like that, who needs enemies?"

iPod giggles.

There is no use in talking to them. I turn around in my seat.

"Hey, Eric?"

Don't look. Don't look. Don't look.

"Eric?"

Don't look. Don't look. Don't look.

"Stop playing, boy. I'm talking to you."

I look. Don't blame me; blame the sudden bass in her voice.

I manage, "Yes? What is it?"

"'*Yes? What is it?*'" Ms. Bazooka mocks. "Damn, boy, you sound white as hell," she says. "Whiter than that boy that kicked your ass before Crash finished you off."

I say, "Benny did not kick my ass."

"Whatever."

"He didn't."

"Did too," she says.

"Did not."

"Did too."

"Did not."

iPod says, "Stop, Chante. This boy will go back and forth with you all day. Lame ass."

They both burst out laughing. Hysterical, sidesplitting laughter. I have to sit here and endure their teasing. As usual, it is all at my expense. iPod's giggle is enough to make me want to do her bodily harm. The passengers around us on the bus are all suddenly interested in our little conversation. A woman in front of me, with dog hair all over her clothes, turns without pretense and eyeballs me. A white man with a priest's collar on the other side of the aisle does the same thing. He looks at me like he wants to sprinkle me with holy water. A woman who looks like a suburban soccer mom can't keep her eyes off me. I wonder why she isn't home baking cookies, why she's even riding the bus. What happened, her minivan is in the shop?

Ms. Bazooka says, "I give you credit."

Stupidly, I ask, "For?"

"Showing your face in public."

I turn away from her again. Turn away from her and iPod's laughter. The bus comes to a stop after some time. A group of people shuffle aboard. They'll be standing, as the bus is completely filled with seated passengers. I look out the window, my thoughts a million miles away. Why does it have to be this way? Out of all the people I could have been born as, why did I end up who I am and with the life I have? What did I ever do to deserve this? There is no peace anywhere in my life. Could it possibly get any worse?

I hear Ms. Bazooka say, "Oh, snap." Then she calls to me, "Hey, Eric?"

I ignore her.

"Hey, Eric?"

I'm not paying her any attention.

The boarding passengers move down the aisle. It's like a mini-stampede. I keep my focus out the window. I don't need to see these new passengers. They're just like everyone else. Certainly not fans of mine, certainly no one who would find any value in me.

"Hey, Eric?" Ms. Bazooka calls for a third time.

I wheel on her. "What? What? What?"

She frowns. "Don't be getting all snappy with me, boy."

I say, "Would you leave me alone?"

Now she smiles. "I was just gonna warn you, but fine...."

"Warn me of what?"

That hateful smile crosses her face again. "That you're probably gonna have to give up your seat."

"You're crazy."

"Am I?"

"Yup."

And then a shadow falls over me. I know the shadow, oddly enough. I swallow a gulp. I don't even have to look up, but I do. I hear iPod's giggle and Ms. Bazooka's laughter in the background. I hear my heartbeat pulsing in my ears, too.

Crash.

Standing over me like the Grim Reaper.

"Hey," I say in a weak voice.

Crash is without emotion. Face blank, eyes dead like they were the day we fought.

Ms. Bazooka says, "Don't be rude, Eric...offer Crash your seat."

I ignore her, ask Crash, "What you been up to?"

He doesn't respond.

My heart does. It wants out of my chest.

My underarms are a pool all of a sudden.

Is he gonna hit me again?

Should I just get up and let him have my seat?

Why isn't he saying anything?

What is he thinking?

Will anyone step forward and be a Good Samaritan if Crash suddenly starts pummeling me?

I say, "Crash, I—"

He cuts me off. "Get up."

iPod giggles. Ms. Bazooka cracks up.

I say, "Come on, Crash. This is my seat."

If I give my seat up, that's just another sad part of this tale. More fodder for the kids at school. I can't give the seat up, no matter how dire the consequences. If Crash decides to beat me up for that, so be it.

"Get up," Crash repeats. His voice is deep, like a grown man's.

I sigh. I won't be moved. He will just have to move me. At some point I have to face down Crash's constant pressure, whatever the outcome, for my own dignity's sake. It's all part of my maturation process. My voice will get deeper, I will grow hair on my chest, and I will stand up to Crash and win. Adolescence.

"Get up," Crash barks.

I can't form my mouth to speak. But I shake my head defiantly.

Ms. Bazooka says, "Oh, snap."

I'd like to snap her neck.

Crash takes a hard step toward me.

I close my eyes and prepare for his assault. I hear every one of his steps. One. Two. Three. He's right on me. I open my eyes, knowing a fist is probably flying toward me.

A fist isn't, though.

But unfortunately, in the same move of opening my eyes, I'd jumped up, jumped up without knowing what was happening.

I say, "Take the seat. I don't want to fight. You have it."

iPod giggles. Ms. Bazooka cracks up.

Crash says, "Your stop."

I look out the window.

It is my stop.

Crash wasn't bullying me. He was letting me know it was my stop.

Again, I punked out, made myself look beyond foolish.

iPod giggles. Ms. Bazooka cracks up.

I move past Crash with my head down.

Exit the bus in the same manner.

I try to sneak into the house without being noticed. Of course that doesn't happen. Mama's in the kitchen, all kinds of wonderful smells around her, and yet she sniffs out my presence like a ninja. "Eric? That you?" Her voice is cooler than the underside of a pillow. It has a jazz singer's strength to it, too. Combine Mama's rich voice with her regal dark skin, Vivica A. Fox frame, and a smile that's more soothing than chicken noodle soup, and you have the adult equivalent of cool.

I must be the only person left on the planet, besides Benny, who doesn't have it.

Despite her calling for me, I try to tiptoe past Mama without answering. I know she'll be at my bedroom door in seconds, knocking and wondering why I passed by without giving her some sugar, but I'll just claim ignorance. *Tired, Mama. Long day. Didn't even hear you in the kitchen. Thought you might have been working late.* That sort of thing.

"Eric Preston Posey, you better bring your narrow tail in here, now."

Dayum.

I turn, head back to the kitchen, a Kanye West I-rule-the-world smile on my face. *Na-na-na-na what don't kill me can only make me stronger.*

I say, "Yes, Mama?"

She looks at me hard, places her hands covered in large oven mitts on her hips, and frowns. "Don't you 'Yes, Mama' me, Eric. You tried to sneak in."

"Sneak in? No."

"Now you're lying to me."

"What's up, Mama?"

"You tell me, Eric."

I shrug my shoulders. "Nothing. Just got in from Benny's."

She glances at the clock, then back at me. "A day early, too."

I forgot that little glitch.

I say, "Forgot I had some work to do here, for school. We had our fun. Now it's work time." I smile for good measure.

Mama cuts her eyes at me. "Dinner will be ready soon. Garlic mashed potatoes. Roasted chicken. Macaroni and cheese. Cabbage with bacon. Honey-topped homemade rolls. Butter pecan ice cream and apple pie for dessert."

I say, "Okay."

"That's every last one of your favorites, Eric. And all I get from you is an 'okay.' No, something's wrong. You're going to talk to me, too, before you even think about leaving this kitchen."

I say, "Did you say 'macaroni and cheese'? I thought you said 'back up off me and leave.' Wow! Mac and cheese, that's great, Mama. Can't wait to dig in."

Mama cocks her head, studies me a moment, and then removes her oven mitts. She moves to the stove, adjusts the temperature on the oven. Turns back to me, points at our kitchen table. I know what this means. A powwow. I move to the table, defeated, find myself a seat. Mama does the same.

She says, "I found a beautiful figurine today. A black peasant woman holding a gourd. Carved in stone. Woman who sold it to me says it's from Norman A. Hughes's Sankofa collection. She sold it to me for a fair price. I'm giving it to Hollywood for his birthday."

I know what she's trying to do. Mama has this thing she does where we sit and discuss the highlight of our day. Most days I have to stretch to find one; today I can't even do that.

I'm not about to play this game.

I focus on Mama instead. Hollywood is her boyfriend. I'm not sure a grown man named Hollywood would appreciate such a gift, but whatever.

I say, "I'm sure Hollywood will love it. He was talking about Yankees tickets, but the black woman holding a gourd is hard to top."

Mama says, "Don't be a smart-ass, Eric."

"What I say?"

"Your tone. You implied that Hollywood isn't astute enough to appreciate a gift of cultural significance."

When you have Mama's type of cool, you can talk like that and not get ridiculed. If you're like me, two steps removed from Steve Urkel, and you talk like that, you risk daily doses of wedgies from the school bullies.

I say, "I wasn't dissing Hollywood. He's cool. Nahmean?"

After my second confrontation with Crash, I'm starting to think Benny was right. I have to reinvent myself.

Mama frowns at the new me. "Since when have you been talking in that manner, Eric?"

I say, "I talk how I talk."

"Ebonics does not suit you. Some things just don't go together. Like that ugly clown rapper with the big clock around his neck and that washed-up blond actress."

"Flavor Flav and Brigitte Nielsen."

"Yes, whoever. Well, dear heart, that's you and Ebonics. Not a good fit."

Mama's right, of course. Sad to say, it's almost more pathetic coming from me than it is from Benny.

I drop my gaze, focus on my shoes. They're nice. Wallabees. Cool shoes, just not on me, I guess. "Sorry, Mama. I don't know what I was thinking."

She doesn't say anything.

But comes to me.

Fingers on my chin lift my head.

Our eyes meet. She looks like she did the day Daddy left for good.

It hits me then. She knows. Knows the struggles I've been having. I've always kept my troubles at school a secret. But Mama, somehow someway, knows.

"I'm a joke, Mama." My voice catches in my throat. It's sad to say, but my eyes start to water.

Mama says, "Oh, Eric, baby. Don't say that. You aren't."

I say, "They hate me. Every last one of the kids at school. Boys. Girls. Doesn't matter. Everybody. They laugh at me all the time. Tease me constantly. I'm the butt of all the jokes."

Big drops of water fall from my eyes. I hate this. I feel so foolish crying in front of my mother. So worthless. The only thing worse would be if I did this in front of the entire school. Can't believe I'm falling apart like this. *Pull yourself together, Eric.*

I can hear them at school: *Cry to Mama. Poser, Poser, Poser.*

Mama says, "Kids can be hateful. But they don't hate you, Eric. They don't understand you. And so they don't appreciate what they don't understand. You just have to get them to understand you. To appreciate you for you." She stops, forces a smile, sniffs out a laugh. "Like how I have to get Hollywood to appreciate a sculpture more than A-Rod and Derek Jeter."

I say, "Just once…" and my voice catches again. I can't get the words from my brain to my tongue. *Just once,* I want to say, *I'd like to be accepted.*

"Oh hells no. I know I ain't seeing what I'm seeing."

Kenya's voice drifts into the kitchen. I try to wipe my eyes. Too late.

Kenya says, "Eric, I know you ain't up in here crying like Paris Hilton going to jail."

Mama says, "Kenya," then, "Correct grammar, girl. It's 'Eric, I know you aren't in here crying like Paris Hilton going to jail.'"

They share a quick laugh.

At my expense, what else?

I make a move to leave.

Mama says, "Eric, hold it. I'm just trying to lighten the mood. Laughter is the best medicine."

Kenya adds, "That's right. If you don't laugh, you'll cry. Oh…wait. You cried already. My bad."

I'm leaving. I make another move.

Mama scolds Kenya, calls me back.

Again, I don't leave.

Mama says, "I'm sorry, baby. I don't quite know how to handle all of this. You'll have to forgive me. My son getting beat up…being so traumatized he has an accident on himself."

I look at Kenya. She told. I can't believe it. The scowl on my face could melt metal.

Kenya obviously isn't metal.

She says, "Who you trying to look at all mean? You better chill, boy."

I say, "I'm not going to be too many more people's *boy* today."

Kenya says, "Look at you getting your panties in a bunch. What happened? Some little old lady punked you today or something?"

She's trying to be funny, and yet has hit the nail so squarely on the head I'm stunned. That's pitiful.

I say, "Go 'head with that," and wave her off.

Something I've heard Crash say.

Mama says, "You two, stop. Eric, your sister was concerned about you. She came to speak to me out of love."

I say, "Whatever. And if I came to you and told you Kenya was using your shower massager for something other than its intended purpose and that she's been seriously contemplating doing the do with a certain boy she often sneaks in the house, would that be love, too?"

Kenya gasps.

Mama says, "Kenya?"

Kenya's nostrils flare. Fire is in her eyes. She says, "Can't believe you went there. You are so lame. That's why nobody can stand you."

Mama is in another place. My words have opened a whole new world of worry in her heart. Now she's worried more about her teenage daughter than her teenage son. Mama's head is no doubt filled with the prospects of grandbabies before their time, that and worse. "Is that true, Kenya?" she asks. "And who is this boy?"

Kenya ignores her. Instead, she directs all her anger at me. "Sometimes I hate you, Eric."

She sounds like she means it.

Mama asks her another question about the mystery boy. Again, Kenya ignores her.

I say, "Sometimes I hate you, too, Kenya. So we're even."

She shakes her head. "I assure you, we aren't. I said *sometimes,* but it's more like *always.* You're an embarrassment to me. I wish you were never born."

I think she's done.

She isn't.

She says, "Crash was considering letting you slide. Came and talked to me about it. You know he's always liked me."

He has.

But Mama would have a fit, and Kenya knows better.

She continues. "I gave him my blessing. Told him to do whatever he had to do to you. I didn't care."

What?

I can't believe what I'm hearing.

Kenya can't possibly hate me that much.

I say, "You didn't. You're just talking."

Mama's completely silent. Lost, I suppose.

Kenya says, "I sure did. I wanted him to beat you up. You do stupid stuff, Eric. And then everybody comes to me with it. And I have to end up cleaning all your messes.

I wanted you to have to clean this up yourself. Teach you a lesson, I hoped."

I open my mouth to speak.

Not for the first time, nothing comes out.

Kenya continues. "I regret it all now, though."

I swallow. There's still a crumb of something between us, at least. I was worried for a moment. All our recent troubles aside, I love my sister. I remember the days when we danced the night away in our pajamas. I remember our games of checkers, tic-tac-toe. All the times we drove Mama crazy playing tag in the house.

Kenya says, "I regret it because then you went and wet... You embarrassed yourself. All everyone talks about." She snarls at me. "And you're *nobody,* so it all falls on me. You being my brother and all. I didn't expect that to happen. Thought you'd have to pay the piper on this one alone."

I'm nobody.

My own sister's estimation of me.

Mama finally comes to life, says, "Oh, Kenya. Take that back. That's a terrible thing to say."

"Terrible, yes, Mama," Kenya admits. "True, though, too."

Mama protests some more.

I finally find my voice. "No need for her to take it back, Mama. She's right. I'm nobody."

Mama says, "Eric, that's not true. Not one bit."

Hollywood walks in then. Wrecks our family moment.

Loud, as usual. He knows no other way to enter a room. "What's up with dinner?"

Mama says, "My children are going through some things."

Hollywood says, "Your children."

He has on his work overalls. His boots are clean. There isn't any dirt under his fingernails. His hands are baby-bottom soft. I feel like exposing his secret to Mama, as well. Let it all hang out today. But I let it go.

Mama, despite all of her tough talk about men to Kenya, moves to finish the dinner preparations.

Hollywood asks Kenya, "So what's happening got all y'all up in here disturbing your mama?"

Kenya is the only other person in the house he speaks to regularly, including Mama.

He practically ignores me.

I don't fit his perception of what a teen boy is, I guess.

Well, he doesn't fit my perception of what a grown man is, either.

So we're even.

He says, "Huh, girl?"

Kenya doesn't answer him. She can't stand Hollywood. She moves past all of us, leaves the kitchen in a huff. Like a gusty wind on a bad day.

Hollywood tells Mama, "That girl's got a serious attitude. You need to check her, Pam. Put her in her place. She in your house running around like she owns the place."

Mama says, "Doing my best." She moves over toward

him, caresses his arms. "Eric is having problems at school. Problems fitting in. Why don't you give him some advice."

No, I want to say. Hollywood isn't an advice giver. I don't want anything from the man, and I certainly wouldn't heed anything he says to me. But I don't say anything. Mama doesn't like it when we say negative things about Hollywood.

Hollywood stares me down for a moment and then says, "Stop being such a pussy. That's my advice."

Some advice.

I leave the kitchen with it.

I don't even hear Mama raise her voice to him.

I told Mama I left Benny's house and came home early because I have a project to work on. That wasn't an outright lie, even though Mama saw through it as if it were as clear as Sprite. It was a partial truth, I admit. I never set out to mislead Mama. Don't have it in me to lie to her. I do have homework. But it isn't for school, as I led Mama to believe. It's for me, a personal project of the highest importance. It holds more weight than anything I've ever done in any of my classes. More important than reading *The Scarlet Letter* in English, fiddling with a Bunsen burner in science, and certainly more important than timing my run of a mile in gym.

The outcome of this project will determine what direction my life takes.

That's how much importance I place on it.

So after I leave Mama and Hollywood in the kitchen, I head straight for my room. Inside, I lock my door, make a call to set up my project, and then move toward the window over my bed. I climb out, just as Ricky Williams does by Kenya's window, and crawl slowly down the side. I'm not cool, true enough. But I'm not afraid of heights, either. I descend smoothly and quickly, too. I'm like Spider-Man if you ask me to scale anything. In some way, I think that must be cool. It feels as if it is, at least. On safe ground at the bottom, I brush off my pants and hands and head to meet up with the person I called to help with my project.

I start walking to our meeting place, wishing the entire time I had an iPod. I have to do something about that soon. I'm a few years away from driving, so everywhere I go is on foot, by public transportation or in the passenger seat of Mama's car. In none of those places am I afforded the opportunity to listen to music I love to hear. Traveling without music isn't good.

When I reach the street of my destination, my palms start to sweat.

Nerves bunch up in my stomach.

What if this doesn't work?

Then what?

I have no options beyond this.

I'll be dead in the water if this fails.

Which means one thing: this has to work.

I look up and notice her coming down the stoop in front

of her apartment. I call her name. She frowns and motions for me to keep walking by. I do. When I reach the corner, I turn back to see if she's following. She is. I smile at the sight of her. *Let the project begin,* I think. As Swizz Beatz says, *Game time.*

"Sorry," she says. "I didn't know if my parental units were looking out the window. They know you're Kenya's brother, but...well, they're protective of me, you know?"

I nod. "Thanks for helping me, Lark. I truly appreciate it."

"I haven't helped yet, Eric. But I will try. I feel bad for you."

"That makes two of us."

She rubs her hands together. "Okay, let's get to work. Favorite book?"

I squint. "Say what?"

"I want to start by asking you some questions. Okay?"

I don't know about this, but I say, "All right."

Lark says, "Now. What's your favorite book?"

"Anything by Baldwin," I tell her. "Oh, and Richard Wright, also. It's too bad we don't read them in school. I loved—"

I stop because I notice Lark is looking at me strangely. She doesn't say a word.

I say, "What?"

"This is going to be hard, Eric. I'll tell you that right now."

"I messed up already?"

She nods. "You answered wrong. And then you started talking about books with enthusiasm. The goal is to be popular, correct?"

I say, "Yes."

"So start over. What's your favorite book, Eric?"

I don't know how to answer. What would a popular boy read? *Harry Potter?*

Lark says, "You wouldn't be caught dead reading a book. *XXL* magazine, maybe *Vibe,* comic books, that's it."

"That's it? No real diversity in what I read?"

Lark sighs. "And if you keep using words like *diversity,* you can forget it."

"You're right. I can't do this." I start to pace the alley we've picked to serve as our classroom. It's cluttered with garbage from the Chinese restaurant out front. A few stray cats move about carefully, their colorful eyes scanning everything that moves around them.

Lark says, "Don't get down on yourself. Let me toss you an easy one. What's your favorite song right now?"

I think about that one for a moment, come up with, "Birdman and Lil' Wayne's 'Pop Bottles' is kind of cool."

Lark smiles, nods and says, "See what I'm saying? You aren't hopeless. It would have been better if you'd said it was *fiyah*, but that's nitpicking."

You aren't hopeless—that's about the best thing I've ever heard.

I say, "Mario's 'Crying Out for Me' is fiyah."

Lark's shoulder's sag; she buries her head in her hands.

I say, "No?"

She shakes her head.

"What's wrong with it?"

She looks up. Says, "Nothing, Eric, unless you're lacking testosterone. If you gotta go R & B, make sure it's something sexual in a bragging way. Stick with R. Kelly and no one else if you get confused. You're a guy. You've gotta act the part. Guys don't like love songs. And if they do, it won't be a sweet love song, it'll be a sexy love song. No emotion involved, just booty. Like R. Kelly." She stops, thinks, and then sings, "'Rubbing on that booty. That booty. That booty.' Okay, Eric?"

"Okay."

She makes a motion. "Walk to that garbage can and back."

I do.

She says, "You need to watch yourself walk in the mirror."

"I have."

"And you still walk like that?"

She must notice the look that comes over my face. She softens her voice, says, "Walking is all about rhythm. Walk like you hear the music from your favorite song playing in your head. Okay?"

I nod, try again.

Her sigh lets me know how I did. She says, "So your favorite song is by Kevin Federline?"

Ouch.

I say, "I'm hopeless."

She says, "No," and looks at her watch. "But I have to head back, Eric. In the meantime, I have an assignment for you."

"Shoot."

"Get out. Observe people. The mall is a good place to observe. You know which boys are cool, which girls are popular. Mimic them. That'll work better than anything I can teach you."

I nod, hold out my hand. She moves beyond it, gives me a hug.

She says, "Take care. Be good."

I watch her move up the street with pep in her step.

Observe and mimic.

I can do that.

sister

sister woke from a deep REM sleep.

She'd been inside a nightmare she never wanted to relive. But she knew she would. Knew she would relive it over and over and over again. What really made that bad was the fact she'd relive it while awake.

She blinked, looked through the darkness of her room. Brother had fallen asleep in her room, as well, again, and lay by the foot of her bed, his CD player's headphones still on, some rapper spitting that nonsense that Brother took as the gospel truth. Brother loved those rappers, lived and would probably die with them. Sister couldn't understand it. Smart as Brother was, how did he get so caught up in some dumb rapper's web? Money, cash, hoes, just as Jay-Z said. All the rappers ever talked about. Sometimes it made Sister sick to her stomach. The girls in the videos, the girls at school, the dudes in the videos, the dudes on the corner, they were all hypnotized in the same way as Brother. They didn't see the bigger picture. The flaws in rap, how it was destroying what little sense of community still existed. The disrespect. The lack of originality. How all the rappers seemed to follow the same beaten path. And Brother idolized them.

Sister slid the earphones off Brother's head, hit the power button on his CD player, eased it away and hopped off the bed. She crossed the room barefoot, placed the CD player carefully on her dresser. Was about to do something when a sound caught her ear. Noises in the house made her jumpy. Any noise in the house scared her, to be honest. That was the sad part of her life, now. She was always on edge about something or other. Especially unexpected noises that were a problem, for sure.

They never led to anything good. They always led to something bad.

She moved to the door, listened intently.

One of Momma's Marvin Gaye albums was playing loud on the stereo. What else? That record was all Momma ever listened to. Or so it seemed. It was good music, though, and Sister could admit as much, even though she was a teenager and every last one of her peers would prefer Young Jeezy to Marvin Gaye any day. Sister wondered where Momma's boyfriend was. He was probably in the bathroom, fussing over the *Star-Ledger*. The sports section first, then everything else in order, starting from page one. He'd stay in there so long his leg would fall asleep. He'd come out, loud, telling it every time. As if it were something to be proud of. I guess when your days were filled with nothing, like his were, anything was a source of pride.

Sister couldn't think of what value he brought to their family.

In fact, all her mind wrapped itself around was the negativity that seemed to follow him.

But there wasn't any use telling any of this to Momma.

Momma was happy.

And blind.

Momma should have been listening to Ray Charles or Stevie Wonder, blind as she was to what was happening under her own roof.

Sister stepped out of her room, headed into the living room. Momma looked up and smiled. Momma was vacuuming, a pot boiling in the kitchen for the dinner she'd be preparing once she'd cleared their threadbare carpet of dirt. Seemed like Momma was always vacuuming, cooking dinner or making excuses for her boyfriend. She was a superwoman for real. Keeping the house going was a juggling act that she'd perfected.

Sister hollered, "What's that playing, Momma?" Joking. She knew the record well.

Momma paused the vacuum's *choom*. "What, baby?"

"What's that playing?"

Momma sort of frowned, said, "My soul on wax, baby," and went right on back to vacuuming.

Sister wasn't in the mood for riddles.

She moved over to the stereo, picked up the album cover for the first time and dusted it off. *Here, My Dear* was the title of the album. Sister wondered what that meant. If she'd taken the time to really listen to the lyrics in the songs, perhaps searched the album title on the Internet to find out more about its recording, she would have found out some things that made what her mother said so much clearer.

Marvin Gaye had completed it after his divorce from Anna.

It was an artistic album, and his poorest seller.

It was about the heartache and pain of an ending love.

It was Momma's soul on wax.

Interesting.

Sister placed the album cover back neatly where she'd gotten it, went back to her bedroom. Brother was just rising from his sleep as she walked in. Seeing him stir made Sister smile. Brother was just about the best thing in her life, even though she'd never admit that out loud. They argued, for sure, but he was her buoy. He kept her from drowning. She was popular in school, unlike him, but that popularity was fool's gold; those same kids who smiled in her face would never be there for her if she ran into any real trouble and needed any real help. Brother would, though, and so she loved him dearly. Not that she'd ever admit any of this to his face.

Wiping his eyes, stretching, yawning, Brother took a

moment to fight off the disorientation that came with just waking up. Then he said, "Why won't Momma turn off that sad record? She keeps playing it over and over again."

Sister said, "Mind your business. Momma can play anything she wants. I like the record myself."

"You would."

"What's that supposed to mean?" Sister was by the bed, her hands balled into fists, ready to pounce on Brother.

"Put your hands down. You ain't doing anything. You *loves* me too much," Brother scoffed. He smirked, turned away.

He was right, of course. What would Sister do without him?

"What's wrong with the record, Brother?"

Brother looked back. "I don't know. It's sad, like I said. Like Tupac's 'Hail Mary.'"

Sister craned her neck, listened. "You can leave," Marvin was singing, "but it's gonna cost you." Sister looked at Brother, nodded. It *was* a sad record. She hadn't picked that up. How had she missed that?

"Quiet other than the record," Brother said. "Where is he?"

"He" was Momma's boyfriend.

"In the bathroom, I think." Sister took a spot on the bed beside Brother, sat cross-legged. A clear sign she wanted to talk.

"Got the paper with him?"

"You know he does. *Star-Ledger*—"

"Sports first, then everything else in order," Brother cut in.

Their mingled laughter was the antithesis of the Marvin Gaye record, full of happiness.

"Don't know what Momma sees in him," Brother said.

"He no-account, ain't he?"

"Definitely is."

"I can't stand the smell of his aftershave. He bathes in that Old Spice."

Brother said, "I don't even get close enough to notice, to be honest. And he doesn't get close to me. Dude acts like I'm not even here."

Sister didn't say anything at that point. Her thoughts took her somewhere else.

Brother said, "You had a million gazillion dollars, what would you do?"

Without hesitation, Sister said, "Give it to Momma. Tell her to buy herself something to make her happy. Something more lasting and stable than him."

"You think money can buy happiness?"

Sister shrugged. "Probably so, maybe it can."

Brother sat back, his gaze across the room. "I'd get out of this place. Buy me a house with no roaches. My own clothes. Enyce. Sean John. Something fly. My shoes'd fit. I wouldn't have to stuff them with newspaper. The halls where I live wouldn't smell like piss."

Sister thought about it. She'd get a steel door for her bedroom and a lock on it that couldn't be picked.

Sister said, "We want the same thing. You just said it different. You said it better than I did."

"Yeah?"

Sister reached forward, clasped hands with Brother. They stayed like that for quite a while.

"You hear that?" Brother asked some time later.

"I don't hear anything."

"Exactly. The record stopped. Come on."

Brother hopped down off the bed, moved hurriedly toward the living room. Sister followed behind him, walking slow, taking her time. Out in the living room, Momma's boyfriend was by the record player, an electrical cord in his hand. He had that angry look in his eyes. Momma was in the middle of the floor, still holding the handle of the vacuum, watching him quietly.

Momma, even in her cheap around-the-house clothes, looked like Beyoncé in *Dreamgirls*. Momma would say Diana Ross from some group named The Supremes that Brother and Sister had never heard of. But whatever.

Even with a shave and a nice hot shower, some new duds, her boyfriend still couldn't pass for this guy named Sam Cooke Momma was always talking about or any of the handsome men in *Dreamgirls*. But whatever.

Momma and her boyfriend were arguing.

Same as always.

"You didn't hear me calling for toilet paper?"

"You know I didn't. I wouldn't leave you sitting in there…"

"Damn music up so loud."

"And the vacuum," Momma replied. "Don't forget the vacuum."

"That supposed to mean something to me, you doing what you supposed to do?"

"Baby…" And Momma stopped at that point, saw Sister and Brother. "Back in the room, you two. This is grown folks' business out here."

Sister and Brother were slow to move.

"Git goin', you heard your mother."

They dashed off at the sound of their mother's boyfriend's voice.

Sister said, "Should have left soon as we seen they were arguing."

"Just because she didn't hear him yelling for toilet paper," Brother said, "he's out there growling like DMX."

"It wouldn't have mattered if Momma did hear him. That was the last roll."

Brother and Sister eyed one another, wished in their silent thoughts for a million gazillion dollars.

"I'm going to see what's happening," Brother said.

"You better stay out of it."

"Just gonna peek."

Brother caught the tail end of conversation. Momma's boyfriend was telling her to go to the store, this time of night, and get some things they needed. And take the boy with you. He'll keep you safe. There were a lot of crazies out there.

Brother came back into the room, closed the door behind him, sat down and started lacing up his sneakers.

Sister said, "What's happening?"

"'Bout to spend the rest of tonight riding buses with Momma. That's what's happening."

"What?"

"He's barking for her to go to the grocery store. And I gotta go with her, keep her safe. I don't know what he thinks I'd be able to do if somebody wanted to get us, but whatever."

Sister said, "At this time of night?" hoping Brother would pick up on the oddity of that.

Brother nodded. "You're lucky. You get to stay here."

Lucky.

Brother didn't get it.

The apartment was dark, much darker than it ever needed to be.

Momma and Brother had been gone only about ten minutes or so. It would take them at least an hour and a half to get to the grocery store and back, and that was if the buses were running on time. The buses never did, though. Sister hated the buses at that moment.

Huddled in bed with her eyes closed tight, Sister tried to think happy thoughts. But then the Marvin Gaye record came on again. Marvin singing that things didn't have to be the way they was, baby. It wasn't actually on, but it was at the same time. In her head, at least.

Sister hadn't locked her bedroom door.

No use.

The lock was cheap and easy to maneuver open. All it took was a screwdriver or knife to pick it. Sister knew. She'd seen it picked with her own eyes. Sat where she was now and seen it picked. Heard the tumblers click open. And then…

Sister started counting backward from one hundred. She'd gotten only as far as fifty-seven when the door creaked open. He stood in the doorway, taking up the entire space with his build, a hateful look on his face. Sister couldn't actually see his face in the dark. But she knew the look was there. It always was. Sister couldn't figure out what Momma saw in him.

"I seen to it they got on the bus, baby girl. It's just you and me now. The way you like it."

He wanted her to say something to that?

"We be alone for a while," he went on. "You and me. Ain't that good, baby girl?"

She stayed silent.

He didn't really care if she ever said a word. It wasn't about that, after all. Wasn't about what she said. Was about what she did. What she allowed him to do. He moved closer, fumbling with his belt buckle. By the time he'd reached the foot of the bed he'd gotten the belt loose, dropped his pants. His jeans pooled around his ankles. He didn't even step out of them. This would be quick, Sister knew. Thank God for that. Thank God this didn't last but a hot minute.

He climbed on the bed and pulled back the covers.

She closed her eyes again.

She felt his rough hands on her skin.

She closed her eyes tighter.

He forced a kiss on her lips.

He was so close, fumbling at her clothes, removing them with little resistance.

"Condom," she said. Her voice was raspy. She'd been crying even before he came in. She knew he'd be coming. "Please," she begged.

"We don't need all that, baby girl," he said.

And that was that. She didn't have any protection, any way you looked at it.

He was in her. Doing his thing.

She closed her eyes and accepted it.

But she'd never accept the smell of Old Spice.

Never.

kenya

I was in a serious Erykah Badu mode.

I had my hair bound in a pretty pink wrap. My torso covered in a sleeveless white top that showed off my flat stomach and nice arms. My Nubian booty sat high and majestic under a soft and beautiful pink wrap skirt. My accessories were on point, too. Sunglasses that looked like Louis V, but with a cost that fit the average Wal-Mart shopper's budget. Birthstone rings on several of my fingers. Tortoiseshell sandals on my feet. A fresh pedicure.

And I moved like music.

"Work ain't honest but it pays the bills."

You could hear those lyrics from "Otherside of the Game" off Erykah's debut CD, *Baduizm,* in my movements. I wasn't being conceited, cocky, any of that. But I swear, as I walked down the sidewalk on my street, drums played to the sway of my hips. Nah, that wasn't conceitedness; it was confidence. Black girls need that. I felt so self-assured. I knew I looked good. I felt even better. I was whole. I had it all. I was doing well in school. God had gifted me with a beautiful singing voice. I had more friends than I could count. And most importantly, I had a boyfriend. And not just any boy, either. I had arguably the most popular boy in school. I had Ricky Williams.

And he was waiting at the end of the street for me. My brother had done his best to shut down my life, make it as miserable as his own, but it hadn't worked. Mama was watching me more closely than usual, but there was only so much she could do. She couldn't keep an eye on me 24/7. She had responsibilities. Like work. She was working then.

I carried a paperback novel in my hand as I walked, clutched against my side like a baby. Terry McMillan's *Disappearing Acts*. Couldn't do Toni Morrison all the time. I'd gotten turned on to the book because of the HBO movie version of the story of Franklin and Zora. Wesley Snipes and Sanaa Lathan in the lead roles. They just happened to be two of my favorite thespians.

There I go again. *Thespians* instead of *actors*. Mama's influence.

Pardon *moi* for that digression.

Anyway.

The book was good.

Real good, as it turned out.

Raunchy and realer than anything I'd ever read.

Grown-up.

What I wanted to be. What I was ready to be.

I was going on my first real date.

Ricky waited patiently, and secretly, in his Honda Accord at the end of my street. He looked as good as me or better. He wore a striped blue and white short-sleeve shirt, baggy jeans and crisp white K-Swiss sneakers. A little too much cologne, but at least it was a pleasing one. Curve for Men.

"You won't be needing that book, Kay."

"Won't need," I corrected him as I closed the door on his ride and buckled my seat belt.

He didn't object to my grammar lesson. He let me be me. That was what I loved most about him.

"What's good?" I asked.

He looked at me with those seductive eyes, licked his lips. "Lot's good, Kay. Lot's good."

I could hear Lark's voice in my head, warning me about giving up the goodies. I wanted that voice silenced. Ricky was so damn fine. Should I? Or shouldn't I? I kept mulling over the choices that were to come. It looked like Ricky was mulling things, too. There was so much passion in the way he looked at me.

I said, "Why you looking at me like that, Ricky?"

"Like what?"

"Like you're a gamer…and I'm Halo Three."

"I'm a what…and you're a who?"

I laughed. "Nothing, boy. Something weird my brother would say. Don't know why I went there."

"Two peas in a pod."

"Whatever, boy."

"That's your brother, Kay. He's a good dude, too. No shame there."

I didn't want to talk about Eric.

I asked, "So what are we doing?"

"Donnell's having a party. Thought we'd hit that."

"Donnell Tucker?"

"Yep."

"You know that boy seriously likes me?"

"Yep. Half the school wants to get with you. So what? You with me."

"You think it's wise to run up in his party with me? He won't like that."

Ricky waved me off. "Donnell's parties are off the hook. We coming out, we gotta do it there. If he trips, he trips."

I'd always heard Donnell's parties were top-notch. His parents had quite a spread, I was told. And they were always out of town. Donnell had the run of the place. But I'd never gone to one of his parties because I knew how he felt about me. It was deep. Two years ago he'd written me the most heartfelt letter. I kept it for six months before I ripped it to shreds. Didn't know why I'd kept it as long as I had. Donnell didn't play sports. He was in all college prep courses. He very rarely came to school dances. It didn't appear that he cared about fitting in. I didn't think he needed to bend his own self in half to be what others wanted him to be, but at the very least he should have shown some concern. He never did. And so I ripped that letter. I couldn't be with someone with such lack of ambition.

I said, "No drama, Ricky."

He nodded, turned up his car's stereo, drove off.

Beyoncé held down the airwaves. She could have had another dude in a minute.

I did my best to ride her voice to a good place.

But I couldn't help feeling uneasy about Donnell's party.

I said, "Wish Lark could have come."

"Can't be having no sophomores up in here. They mess the vibe up. And especially Lark, with her young-acting self."

Sad to say, I didn't even put up a fight.

She had said I'd forget her.

I hadn't. But close.

We parked at the end of Donnell's street and walked to his house. Ricky held my hand, which set me somewhat at ease. The street was lined with vehicles. Shiny rides the colors of fruits, adorned with sparkling rims and tinted windows. There was no question we'd arrived at party central. It was easy to tell which house was Donnell's. It was lit up like a Christmas tree. Loud music from inside pierced the air. Several people milled around outside on the lawn. I could only imagine what the neighbors were feeling. Luckily, it was a mixed crowd. A regular United Nations. I spotted two Asians, more than a few whites, even an Indian girl. If it had been an all-black affair, I couldn't help thinking, the police would have been there to shut it down.

"There's Diddy's white party in the Hamptons," Ricky said, "and then there's this."

"Now you're being dramatic."

Ricky nodded thoughtfully. "You'll see."

And I did.

Donnell's party was tight. I had to hand it to him.

He had a DJ and everything. DJ Skills. He was a thin dude with dreadlocks down to his shoulders, an easy smile and magic hands. He didn't just spin records; he became one with them. He had everyone at Donnell's party entranced. A serious crowd pleaser, that DJ Skills. And he totally played into the hype of the moment. The whole hip-hop world was watching Kanye and 50 Cent. Skills ate that up. He played a Kanye record. Then a Fif. Back to back to back to back. There was a fever in Donnell's basement, and it had a hold on everyone. I fell in love with Ricky at that moment. All over again. He'd brought me there. He'd introduced me to a little slice of heaven. All night long I was either squeezing his hand, kissing his cheek and lips or running my fingers over his head.

When "Stronger" stopped playing, "I Get Money" seamlessly filled its space.

Everyone erupted like a volcano.

"Oh my God," I said to Ricky.

"I know," was all he could say in return.

All the uneasiness I'd felt earlier was gone.

I missed Lark's presence less and less with each pass-ing second.

"How long you two been kickin' it?"

That was Donnell.

Ricky and I were chilling on a couch in the corner of Donnell's humongous basement. Donnell was resting on the couch's arm, sipping a red drink that looked like fruit punch. I'd stayed away from the punch because I'd heard rumors about what it really contained. But the bug was biting me. It wasn't going to be long before I was sipping some punch myself. Call it peer pressure. Assimilation. Whatever. I wanted some of that punch myself.

Ricky said, "Can't even call it. Even when we weren't together...we were. If that makes sense. Kay's my heart. Always has been. Always will be."

My heart swooned at those words. They were even more heartfelt than the words Donnell had written to me in that old letter.

Donnell had a constipated look on his face, but he managed to push out, "Kay *is* something special."

Ricky just squeezed my hand. I wanted to elbow him in the side, signal to him that he should ease up on the lovey-dovey around Donnell. Donnell wasn't looking too good. It was all over his face. He couldn't even hide his disgust. Boy looked like he needed a shot of insulin or something.

Ricky said, "Kay is one in a million, dawg. And out of all the dudes trying to holla...she chose me."

Donnell nodded. "She chose you."

I said, "Y'all talking like I ain't even here."

I admit it, *ain't* replaced *I'm not* and such when I was around my peeps.

Ricky said, "DJ Skills is nice."

Donnell replied, "He's got a baby by one of my cousins. He hooks me up because we're basically family."

I said, "Okay. I guess I'm *not* here," and got up. "Where's your bathroom, Donnell?"

He smiled a smile that wasn't a smile and pointed toward the stairs on the other side of the room. "Upstairs. Hang a right. Straight down the hall. You can't miss it."

Four more people entered our space.

Mustafa Coles. His on-again-off-again girlfriend, loudmouthed Renee. Doug Draper. And a kid everyone called Chuck because his teeth were big enough to carve sculptures out of logs. My bladder was about to burst, but I couldn't move right then. I had to stay by my man and represent for a little while first.

Loudmouthed Renee said, "This party is ridiculous, Donnell."

He nodded thanks. Kept his eyes on me. I wondered if anyone else noticed.

Chuck said, "That was crazy when he kept playing Kanye and Fifty back to back."

Ricky said, "I bet you were loving Fif, huh, Chuck?"

Chuck scowled. "What's that supposed to mean?"

Ricky shrugged.

Chuck said, "You clownin' me, Ricky?"

Loudmouthed Renee said, "He sure is. You know you and Fifty Cent got the same big-ass teeth, boy. I got a rhyme for Mr. Vitaminwater's ass. How much wood could a woodchuck chuck if a woodchuck could chuck wood? You feel me?"

Everyone laughed at Renee's lame joke. Even I did. Nothing could kill your popularity quicker than swaying from the crowd. If everyone laughed, you'd better laugh. If everyone rushed the dance floor for a certain song, you'd better be out there shaking your ass with them. That was just how it went.

Chuck said, "When I'm in the NBA making that paper that's out of this world…y'all can kiss my asteroid."

Loudmouthed Renee said, "Corny."

Chuck had the width of a number two pencil but was built tight with muscle. His b-ball skills were legendary. One of the stars of the school's team. He held the school's record for total career points. And he'd bested the old mark at some point during his junior year. A local sports-writer had compared him to George "Iceman" Gervin. Whoever that was.

I loved being with this cool crowd, but my bladder was ready to beat me like Juanita Bynum's husband if I didn't empty it pronto. I asked Donnell, "Hang a right, straight down the hall?"

He nodded. His eyes burned a hole in me.

I told Ricky to get me a fruit punch and excused myself.

DJ Skills was playing a Keyshia Cole record. Somebody yelled out, "You got her hands down, Kenya."

I didn't turn to thank whoever for the compliment.

I was on a mission for that bathroom.

Donnell's parents had a really nice place. As bad as I had to wee-wee, I still took a minute for a quick peek around the upstairs. The dining room, living room and kitchen could have been featured in an *Ebony* magazine spread. Pictures of Donnell were everywhere. I wouldn't hold that against his parents, though. Truth be told, he was a good-looking guy. Not on par with Ricky, but close enough to make some girl happy.

I thought of Lark, then. I was so confused. I did miss my girl. Wished she were there. Maybe I could use the pull I had over Donnell to convince him to let her come next time. She was the coolest of the cool, as far as I was concerned. She'd liven up the party even more.

But I digress.

I finally stopped looking around Donnell's home and went to handle my business in the bathroom, which smelled better than any bathroom should. Some kind of berries 'n' vanilla scent. It was decorated in soothing pastel colors. A magazine rack held enough reading material for a lifetime. I skimmed a *Jet* article about my favorite actor, Terrence Howard. He was a talented and passionate brother. He spoke in the article about wanting to win back his ex-wife's heart. I put the magazine down at that point. For some reason it made me think of Ricky's ex, Monique. I hadn't thought about her in some time. I didn't need that downer.

I washed my hands with lavender soap, touched up the little makeup I wore—mostly lipstick and a bit of eye shadow—and headed back out.

I didn't immediately realize that someone was in the semidark hallway with me.

Until I heard a voice.

"He's gonna play you."

I touched my chest, felt my heartbeat pulsing like a drum. "What's wrong with you, Donnell? You scared me silly."

Donnell stepped from the shadows. He handed me a plastic cup of fruit punch. I didn't take it, and yet he didn't withdraw his hand. I ignored all that. I looked toward the door that led to the basement. I wanted to be downstairs with my boo.

Donnell, reading my mind, it seemed, said, "Ricky ain't move from his spot. So I went ahead and got your drink for you. Here, take it."

I took it from him without saying thanks. Good party or not, I wasn't about to be gracious.

"You're welcome, Kay."

"Don't call me that."

"Oh? Only Ricky can get that?"

"That's right."

"He's gonna play you."

"Don't hate just 'cause I don't want your tired ass."

"I'm not worried about that," he said, waving me off dismissively.

"Whatever."

"You'll be a free agent again soon enough. Ricky don't hold on to anyone but so long."

I thought about Monique again. She'd seemed so comfortable with Ricky that day Lark and I had seen them at the mall. And worse, Ricky had seemed so comfortable with her. But here I was, with him, less than a week after that scene.

I told Donnell, "It's different with me."

"Is it? That's really what you think? I feel sorry for you."

"You can forget about me being a free agent anytime soon."

"When it happens, and it will, don't come crying to me, Kay."

"I said don't call me that."

He put his hands up. "Don't want to upset you. I'm just glad you came. I've been throwing these parties for two years, hoping one day you'd walk through my door. Alone, of course. I never figured Ricky in my dreams."

At that I pushed past him and headed for the door to the basement. I didn't want to hear all that romantic mumbo jumbo. I had my hand on the doorknob. I was an inch away from being out of his presence. Sometimes an inch might as well be a mile.

"Kenya?"

I wish I'd ignored him. But I didn't.

I wheeled around to face him. "What, boy?"

"Girl Monique that Ricky was dealing with…"

"What about her?"

"Heard her moms pulled her out of school and sent her down south somewhere."

"So?"

"Her moms, my moms, your moms, they're from the same generation, the same time."

"So?" I didn't understand where he was going. Didn't want to really understand.

"So," Donnell said, "my moms told me that's what they used to do to girls back in the day when they got pregnant."

He disappeared into the shadows before I could reply.

Left me standing there with a million unanswered questions.

"Thanks, baby. I needed that. That party was it."

Ricky smiled, nodded. "I told you, Kay. Donnell does it up."

I couldn't just jump right in and ask the question that was really on my mind. I had to tread carefully. Use strategy. But boy, did I want to just blurt it out.

Ricky was idling by the curb outside Donnell's place.

I said, "We can chill, Ricky. You don't have to take me right home."

Ricky looked over at me with something animal in his expression. I straight brought out the gorilla in him. I wondered if he'd ever looked at Monique in the same way. Then I tossed that thought aside. Of course he had.

I just knew.

Ricky said, "You're mine? You don't have to get home?"

I reached over, found a comfortable resting place for my head on his shoulder. "Baby, I'm all yours. My mama's working the graveyard."

"Where you wanna go?" The excitement in his voice was next level.

"Somewhere quiet where we can be alone."

"Word."

"And talk."

"Talk?" Ricky looked like Kanye West the night he put President Bush on blast. He wasn't happy. And he couldn't hide the fact. That made me feel some kind of way. My boyfriend didn't want to talk to me. That left only one thing he did want to do with me.

I repeated, "Talk."

"I don't have much to talk about, Kay. It's been a long night."

That moment in my bedroom, Ricky reciting the Toni Morrison passage to me, it seemed like years ago. That disappointed me. I wanted to believe the best about Ricky. Our situation was too new for me to be having these problems, these doubts. I hated doubt. And I was full of it. But Donnell had kicked a rock and jarred loose an army of hungry ants. They needed to be fed as badly as I needed answers. There was no turning back now.

I asked Ricky, "So what happened to your ex? I heard she moved."

Ricky frowned. "My ex?"

Playing dumb. I didn't like that at all. More points deducted.

I said, "Your tall friend...Monique."

He shrugged, took his gaze off of me and started playing with his cell phone. He had a Sidekick. All of a sudden it was the most important thing in his world. He started thumbing text messages to someone like text messaging was going out of style, as my mother would have said. I wasn't even in the car with him anymore. I was an afterthought. Forget the cell phone; I wanted to be his only sidekick.

I said, "Ricky?" in my sweetest voice.

"Holeup, Kay. Donnell's hitting me up."

Donnell was the source of my impending pain. I hated him. I wished he would disappear like Karl Kani clothes.

I said, "What that fool want?"

Ricky didn't answer.

"Ricky?"

"Said holeup, Kay."

He stayed busy typing with his thumbs. Mama always told me a smile and a quick batting of the eyes was enough to turn any man from any emotion back to love, or at the very least, lust. I reached over and gently took the Sidekick from Ricky's hands. He turned on me, surprised and obviously angry. I smiled and batted my eyes. When I saw his shoulders ease, I plugged his cell phone into the cigarette lighter so it could charge.

Ricky sighed long and hard. Seemed to consider something and then said, "Okay, Kay. What are we talking about? I see you ain't gonna let me chill."

"Monique."

Ricky sighed again. Long and hard, of course. "I left her for you, Kay. I'm done with that situation. What we need to talk about her for?" His forehead was lined like that of a man three times his age. Worry was in his eyes. His posture was tense. There were probably knots in his neck.

I wouldn't let this all go, though.

I said, "I heard she moved suddenly. You know where?" I paused to let my next thought sit on its own. "You know why?"

"No and no. Now drop it."

Like I said, I had to tread carefully. Use strategy. I glanced at Ricky's cell phone in the cigarette-lighter charger. Then I looked at Ricky. I smiled and batted my eyes. "I'm sorry. I'm tripping."

"You are, Kay. You know it's all about you. You and only you. Apple of my eye and all that jazz."

He was laying it on too thick. But whatever.

I said, "Thought I said let's go somewhere we can be alone."

"Shoot, you don't have to tell me twice."

Ricky put his key in the ignition. R. Kelly's song was

probably playing in his head. That was too bad. He'd blown it and didn't even know it. Ricky Williams probably would never get to put his key in my ignition. I was a mixture of sad and angry.

"This night is gonna end on a beautiful note, Kay. It's gonna be lovely."

A 50 Cent Negro trying to talk like Will Smith. Yeah, he definitely thought he was getting my goodies. Wasn't happening.

"Stop at the 7-Eleven."

Ricky stopped the car but didn't pull in. "For what, Kay?"

"So you can run inside and get me a Slurpee."

"You're kidding, right?"

"You don't want to get your baby a Slurpee?"

"I want to get somewhere alone with my baby."

I leaned over and kissed him with all the bottled-up passion inside me. I loved him and I hated him. He had me so twisted up. I was an emotional pretzel thanks to this boy.

When I pulled back from the kiss, Ricky said, "What flavor?"

"Surprise me."

He pulled into the lot and jumped out before his car stopped moving. He wanted my goodies in the worst way. He would do just about anything to get at me. I waited until he was safely inside before I picked up his cell phone and scrolled through his contacts list. I found Monique's number with little trouble and saved it into my phone. There was also another number with Monique's name attached to it. In the contacts it was named *MoniquesCuz*. I saved that one as well. Then I checked for Ricky's text messages.

He had none.

He must have deleted them as soon as they came through.

Just another reason I had to leave this situation alone.

But that was going to be difficult. Ricky was my drug.

I put the phone back in place when I noticed Ricky inside the 7-Eleven at the counter. He paid and headed back outside, one hand behind his back as he moved toward the car. He walked toward me with the biggest smile on his face. I wished I could return the smile but I couldn't. My insides were churning.

He slid in the driver's side, closed the door.

I forced a stricken look, said, "My mother just called me. She wants me home. Now."

The smile left Ricky's face. "Thought she was working. How she find out you were out?"

"Don't know. Maybe my brother told. He is a hater."

Ricky said, "Kick his lil' narrow…" but let the thought drift.

He was disappointed and angry. I wondered which emotion would eventually dominate. One had to.

I reached over and touched his leg. "Some other time, baby."

He put my Slurpee in a cup holder, dropped a single rose on the console between us. The rose was what he'd had behind his back.

Any other time I would have been excited.

Other things were on my mind then.

Monique, for the most part.

But I didn't lose sight of one fact as I reached over and picked up my Slurpee cup: that was the second time that night Ricky hadn't handed me my drink.

Ricky pulled onto my street. Parked at the end. He left his engine running. He didn't look in my direction.

I said, "Penny for your thoughts."

He hadn't spoken the entire ride.

"Dunno. Ain't really got none, Kenya."

Kenya.

"You don't *have* any," I said, correcting his grammar.

"Yeah, whatever you say, Kenya."

All the love was gone from his voice. I wasn't Kay any longer. I was Kenya.

"Are you upset, Ricky?"

"Why would I be upset? Because my girlfriend has to be home before Power 105.1 stops playing hip-hop and puts on slow jamz? Because I thought my girlfriend was gonna actually *act* like a girlfriend tonight? No. Not me."

"What do you mean 'act like a girlfriend,' Ricky? Give you some? That's what it's all about?"

"You know it ain't all about that, Kenya. But that's important. Don't sleep on that."

"Let's talk about this."

He shook his head. "Go on in the house. We talked

about this when we were kicking it before. I'm tired of talking about it. That's why I lef—"

He caught himself.

"Go ahead and finish it, Ricky. That's why you left before. That's why you hooked up with Monique. I don't have sex with you and you start tripping. That's all that matters to you."

"Don't matter, Kenya."

"Doesn't," I corrected, pushing my luck, I knew.

Then it happened.

He looked at me in a manner I'd never seen before. The distance between us at that moment couldn't even be measured in miles. I should have been happy, considering all I suspected regarding Ricky and Monique. But I wasn't. I still loved the boy. Too much.

He said, "I gotta go. So do you, Kenya."

I leaned over to kiss him. He turned away. I still planted one on his cheek.

I got out of the car, closed the door and leaned down to speak through the passenger-side window. "Call me?"

He looked at me for a brief moment without speaking and then put the car in drive. I leaned away so he wouldn't decapitate me as he pulled off. At least one of my questions was answered: anger was the more dominant of his emotions.

I stood at the curb and watched his taillights wink at me as he got to the end of my street. He turned left.

I swallowed a pound of regret.

The way to his place was right.

I turned and looked at my own place. I didn't want to go inside. I really didn't. As difficult as things were outside, they were even more difficult once I walked inside. Life was difficult. Life was troubling. Sometimes life didn't feel worth living.

Mama was right.

I'd messed up big-time.

I'd given my heart to a boy.

And he'd broken it.

Eric

"**I'm** tryin' to put you to bed...bed...bed. I wanna put you to bed...bed...bed."

I can't stop staring at the pretty young thang singing those lyrics at the Suncoast Video store in the mall. She's more beautiful than anything that I could ever put into words. And dressed to kill. True Religion jeans so tight they look like they'll burst if she takes a deep breath, a formfitting pink T-shirt, Steve Madden boots, a pink Yankees fitted cap on her head. She's Lisa Raye-brown, with hazel eyes and the body of a fully developed woman. A healthy and desirable fully developed woman. The kind you see in *King* and *XXL* magazines or 50 Cent videos. I'm glad I listened to Lark's advice to get out to the mall. Staying cooped up in my house to avoid people certainly isn't the answer. I can run but I can't hide from my lack of cool. I had to get out of the cave also known as my bedroom. And this girl is beautiful enough to get Osama bin Laden out of the hills of Afghanistan. Only bad thing: I haven't gotten a chance yet to observe some cool boys in action, as Lark suggested. If I go in, it'll be cold.

"Take you to bed, bed, bed."

Pretty as can be. But she can't hold a tune. A fact I won't hold against her. She's probably better than I'm giving her credit for. But then, I compare everyone's singing to my sister's, and Kenya can't be touched in that department. As much as we butt heads, that I can't take away from her.

"Take you to bed…bed…bed," Pretty Young Thang sings.

Her audience, other than me, is the poor sales associate scheduled to work today. The sales associate is so pale I want to donate a couple pints of blood to her. Short black hair frames her face. Not sure who snipped her locks, but whoever it was, they were either blind or aspiring to be. Her hair is a zigzagging, uneven mess. Her fingernails are just as black as her hair. I think she's going for the goth look. She missed. She says, "And you say it's called 'Take You to Bed'?"

Pretty Young Thang says, "Don't know what it's called. I'm asking you. That's how the chorus goes, though."

"Sing it again."

I want to say *Please don't*. But I don't. I just continue to stare at Pretty Young Thang.

Pretty Young Thang sighs. Sings it again.

"And who's the artist?" asks the sales associate.

Pretty Young Thang looks like she's about to turn into a Southern preacher and lay hands on the sales associate.

I clear my throat, move away from the bin of CDs I've been going through. Leave behind the MIMS CD I've been mulling over. In my mind MIMS is providing a sound track of courage for what I'm about to do. I keep telling myself *This is why I'm hot.*

I move tentatively, stop next to Pretty Young Thang, say, "'Bed.' J. Holiday."

She turns, eyes me. The wrinkle girls always seem to get in their noses when I come around doesn't appear. She says, "Excuse me? What?"

My voice cracks as I say, "That song you were singing. I heard you. Sorry I eavesdropped. It's called 'Bed.' The artist's name is J. Holiday."

"Shut up." She touches my arm. "Are you for real? You know it?"

"Yep."

I try to stay calm. I can still feel the spot where she touched my arm. It scorched me. This girl is hotter than the sun.

She smiles. "Fell in love with it the first time I heard it. Always seem to catch it on the radio at the end, never got the title or the artist."

The sales associate drifts away. Back to the bat cave, I suppose.

I nod at Pretty Young Thang. "It's a hot song. It'll be rotational before you know it. Twenty or thirty times a day you'll be hearing it on the radio."

Pretty Young Thang asks, "What stations you listen to?"

"Hot 97. Power 105.1. But Hot 97 mostly."

She nods herself, smiles. Her smile is a sunrise, a sunset, any- and everything beautiful that God created. She says, "I love Hot 97. Angie Martinez is my girl."

I volley, "Don't forget Funkmaster Flex."

"Mornings aren't mornings without Miss Jones."

"DJ Envy... Envy."

"Ed Lover down the dial," she says. Down the dial is Power 105.1.

"DJ Clue."

I could go on naming radio personalities with her for the rest of my days.

She pauses, says, "Endia Patton."

I frown. "Don't know her. Is she on Hot or Power?"

Pretty Young Thang laughs, flips her hair. "That's me, silly. My name's Endia."

"Oh." I regroup. "Oh, okay."

Silence settles between us.

She says, "And you are...?"

"I am..." Drawing a complete and utter blank.

She raises her eyebrows as if to say *And?*

"Eric Posey," I manage. I've only lived with the name for fifteen years; forgetting it is understandable. Right?

She says, "I just realized something. *EP.* Our initials match, Eric. How cool is that?" She touches my arm again. I'm feeling light-headed. I need a dose of oxygen.

I say, "Thought you said your name was India?"

"It is. With an *E,* though. Don't ask. My mother is a creative soul."

"I like that. Endia with an *E*."

She asks where I go to school. I ask the same of her. She asks what grade I'm in. I ask the same of her. Basically she is driving the conversation. I'm worse than our president. Bushwhacked by Endia's beauty. Not one original thought do I have.

Endia says, "So where do you be at, Eric?"

"Where do I be at?"

"Where do you hang out? What do you do?"

I stop and think about Crash and all the other popular boys at school, how they'd answer. Come up with, "Blockbuster used to be my joint, but Moms shut that down, went and got Netflix."

Endia looks puzzled for a moment, but then a smile spreads across her gorgeous face. "You're funny bad, Eric."

Funny.

I was trying for suave.

Missed that like the entire season of *I Love New York*.

Endia says, "So I won't see you anywhere unless I camp out by the post office?"

"The post office?"

She says, "When you mail back those Netflix videos."

"Oh." I laugh. Regroup for the ninety-ninth time. Unlike Jay-Z, I've got ninety-nine problems. And a girl is one. I add, "I come through the mall a couple times a week."

Come through. I've heard Crash say that enough that I know I must get that in.

Endia says, "Me, too. I'm either up in the food court

at Chik-Fil-A, at Loews playing video games or seeing a movie, or over at the Verizon store fussing with them about some problem or other with my cell phone." She takes out her cell phone. It's an LG Chocolate. But pink.

I say, "Nice phone."

She hands it to me, says, "It's real sensitive. Go ahead and type in your number and see for yourself."

I take it, type in my number, then quickly slide it closed and hand it back to her. "You're right. It is sensitive. But it's a cool phone."

Endia looks at me again with that puzzled look.

Then I see it.

Her nose wrinkles.

I'm like the opposite of a Botox injection.

Instead of making wrinkles go away, I make them appear.

Endia says, "It was nice meeting you, Eric. I've got to get going… Maybe I'll see you around."

"I'll look for you."

She frowns, nods, says, "Thanks again."

"For?"

"'Bed.' J. Holiday. I've been going crazy trying to figure out who sings that."

"You would have found out eventually, Endia. It's gonna get a lot of burn on the radio."

Burn. Something else I've heard from Crash.

Endia says, "Yeah. That's what's up."

"Yep. So I wasn't that big of a help."

She cocks her head to the side, studies me briefly, then says, "Guess you weren't, then, Eric."

She moves away without another word. I watch her go. Her walk is like that Tony Yayo song: so seductive. There was so much I wanted to ask her, but didn't. It all comes to me now. There were traces of something exotic in her look, something more than black, and I wanted to ask her about it. She smelled like heaven. I wanted to ask her what perfume she was wearing, too. What type of music did she like? Just R & B? Was she into rap? Who were her favorite artists?

A full minute after she's gone I'm standing in the same place, looking in the same direction. The direction she disappeared into.

A hand touches my shoulder, interrupts my reverie, a baritone voice says, "That was painful to watch, son."

It isn't my father.

So *son* must be cool-speak.

I say, "How you figure, son?"

"You gotta ask?"

I turn to place a face with the voice.

Black guy. Late twenties, I'd guess, maybe younger. His lopsided beard probably makes him look older than he actually is. He dresses like the dudes in my school. Baggy gray jeans, Timbs, a Howard U sweatshirt, real Louis Vuitton sunglasses, fitted baseball cap he's got on in the fashion of T.I., Jay-Z and all the other rappers who sport baseball caps in their videos. You know, cocked at a severe angle on their head.

I say, "I gotta ask."

He shakes his head. "Shorty was practically throwin' you the panties. And you fumbled. Fumbled bad. You was like Tiki Barber them first coupla years."

He has a rich baritone, a familiar voice that sets me at ease like chicken soup. I want to talk to him even though Mama burned it into my brain to never ever talk to strangers.

I ask, "How I fumble?"

"How you didn't?"

"School me." Maybe he can impart something to me that Lark couldn't.

He laughs. "See, that right there. You didn't say nothin' even close to that cool the whole time shorty was over here." He shakes his head in disappointment.

I repeat, "School me."

He says, "Swagger, son."

"What about it?"

"You gots to get you some."

"How?"

"Wish I could direct you to eBay or Amazon.com. But alas..." And he laughs at his choice of words, a phrase I want to tell him isn't cool enough for someone with his obvious swagger. "But seriously. I feel you, though, son. I was somewhat lacking at your age, too. Can it be that it was oh so simple then?"

I say, "Wu-Tang."

"What?"

"'Can it be that it was oh so simple then?' Reminds me of Wu-Tang."

He says, "You're young. You remember the Wu?"

I nod. "Are you kidding me? I loved those cats. Meth. Ghostface. Raekwon. Masta Killa. U-God. Inspectah Deck. RZA. Ol' Dirty, RIP."

"So you a hip-hop head?"

"Yep. I consider rappers to be our modern-day poets."

He nods, says, "Twentieth-century Paul Laurence Dunbars."

That stuns me into silence for a moment.

After a moment I say, "You know Paul Laurence Dunbar?"

"I do." He says that matter-of-factly. As if everyone should know him. And everyone should, I agree, but few do.

"I've never met anyone who did."

"You haven't gotten around much."

"I guess."

"You remember Arsenio Hall?"

"Who?"

He smiles. "Dating myself. Anyway, Arsenio had the hottest show on late-night television. Maya Angelou was on once. She recited a Paul Laurence Dunbar poem. Performed it like a rap. She was great. Coolest older woman you ever saw. She had Arsenio's young audience eating out of the palm of her hand."

"Wow!"

"But enough of that. We need to talk about that shorty."

"So what I do wrong with Endia? Tell me exactly."

He starts ticking off offenses with his fingers. Runs out of fingers and starts again at finger one. "Your first opportunity to impress was when she asked your name. It took you a minute to even remember it. Not good. And, son, you need to have a nickname or something to liven that up, too. *My name's Eric, but everyone calls me E-double*. You got it?"

I nod.

He goes on. "She thought the fact your initials matched hers was the new Apple iPhone, son. You should have played that up. *The moon, sun and stars are aligned with us, ma*. You got it?"

Another nod from me.

"She gave you her phone to save your number in. You didn't. You typed it in and then just shut her phone without saving the number. I almost shitted my pants on that one, son. I kid you not."

I say, "That's why she gave me that funny look?"

"Yeah, son."

"Dang."

"And," he continues, "she acted like you threw down your coat over a puddle because you knew the name of that song. Then you played yourself by acting like it was no big deal. Humble is good, son, but I would have played that to my favor. For real. Acted like I came up with a plan for us to pull out of Iraq or somethin'. Said something like, *You know I got you, ma*."

I roll that off my tongue. "You know I got you, ma."

"That's it."

"Okay. I think I understand."

He says, "So you like hip-hop?" The redirection in the conversation is abrupt, but I move right along with him.

"Definitely," I acknowledge.

He asks, "Who you feelin'?"

I say, "Eclectic taste."

"School me," he says, smiling.

"Nas. Common. When I want to be fed."

He nods. "That's what's up."

"LL manages to stay relevant. My mother was rocking him back in the day and he's still at it."

"Word. Word. LL means Living Legend, you ask me. I feel that."

I say, "Fifty gets a lot of criticism, but I think a lot of what he does is entertaining. And I admire his hustle."

"Okay."

"Lil' Wayne is ridiculous right now. He said it best himself. 'I am a beast.'"

"He's on his grind. I ain't mad at him."

I say, "T.I. Young Jeezy. Young Dro. Young whoever. The South is blazing."

He nods. "You couldn't hold 'em down with a Master Lock and chains."

I've heard that before. I flip through my mental Rolodex. Then recollection takes shape. Heard that line in a rhyme. *My style is long-range. You couldn't hold it down with a Master Lock and chains.*

I say, "Fiasco. He's got a line like that in one of his songs."

He smiles deeper than ever. "You like that cat?"

"Fiasco's underrated. I heard a leak of this new song he has coming out on the Internet. Can't tell you how many people have it on their MySpace pages. It's a hit, for sure. He's going to be so large when it hits radio. One of the best lyricists in the game. He sounds so comfortable on his records, like he's at peace with the beats."

He says, "Swagger, son. Swagger."

I'm about to agree when I realize something. The baritone. The familiarity of his voice. I say, "Could you remove your shades for a moment? I want to see your eyes. This is so impersonal."

"What?" he says through a deep frown. That lopsided beard becomes even more lopsided when he frowns.

I repeat a Dipset line to set him at ease. "No homo."

He pauses, removes the shades quickly and puts them back on just as quickly.

I'm stunned.

So much I missed in this encounter.

Most notably the tattoo inked on his neck. You can see the edges of it over the collar of his shirt. It's in the shape of the state of New Jersey, with a microphone cord wrapped around it like a snake. The Dirty Jersey clique's official tattoo. That clique is rapper Fiasco's famous entourage.

I'm so stunned I can't move, speak or get my thoughts together.

I'm standing next to Fiasco.

He sees the realization set in my eyes.

Nods.

Holds out his hand.

I grip it weakly.

He grabs mine tighter, pulls me into a ghetto shoulder hug.

I come out of the hug with something in my hand.

A small square of paper.

I look at it, befuddled.

He says, "My business card. That number is my own private and personal line. You can get me at any time with that number. Just don't abuse it. And it's for your eyes only. I don't need a bunch of little *106 and Park*-watching young heads blowing me up."

I look him in the eyes. "Why?"

He pats my shoulder. "You aiight, Eric. And I like to keep up with what's happening with the young heads. Young heads drive hip-hop." He pauses, looks at me. "If you've got your finger on the pulse, Eric, you can help me."

"How?"

"Keep me relevant...like you said about LL. Let me know what's popping off with the young heads. What clothes is the shit. What songs they feeling. The newest slang. Et cetera, et cetera. You can do that? You got your finger on the pulse?"

I couldn't feel the pulse if it were beating with the arrhythmia of a heart attack.

But I know Crash and others who do. So I say, "I got you, Fiasco."

"Cool. That's what's up."

He turns to leave. I call after him. He turns back.

He says, "Yo?"

"One bit of advice from me."

"Shoot."

I point to his chin. "You need a better disguise. That beard is terrible."

He smiles, and then laughs. The beard dances as he laughs. "Good looking. Hit me up," he says, and then he's gone.

kenya

I'd tried Monique's number several times. All it did was ring endlessly. It didn't even cycle over to voice mail. I was beyond frustrated. The universe didn't want me to find answers, I guessed. I was left with nothing but questions. And only one person I knew of who truly had the answers to those questions: Ricky. And he wasn't about to help me out.

What next?

I hadn't spoken more than a few strained words to Ricky in a couple days. He was being as difficult as a so-called boyfriend could be. I was wounded by his disses. I didn't want to be, but I was. And something had to give. I had to find out some truths and then take it from there. Maybe my suspicions about Ricky and Monique were wrong. If that was the case, then I'd apologize to Ricky until I turned blue in the face, and yes, I'd gladly give him the goodies.

But there I was, stuck.

And then I remembered, stupid me, that I had a second number attached to Monique.

I searched my phone contacts and found it. *MoniquesCuz.*

I dialed.

It rang.

I crossed my fingers.

And on the fourth ring I heard, "Who dis?"

I cleared my throat. "Yo. Where Monique at?"

"Who dis?" again.

"This Kenya. Where Monique?"

"Y'all need to stop blowing up my phone trying to get at my cousin. I ain't even talked to her my own self. Not since all the drama went down."

Cuz. It all made sense then. And what drama was he talking about?

I said, "I'm saying."

Say little and hope he says much, that was my creed.

He said, "You that bird was with her at the party last month?"

I lied, "Yup."

His tone changed. "You got a fatty, girl. What's up with you?"

"Trying to get my jeans back. Homegirl took my joints and I ain't heard or seen her since."

He was quiet. I must have messed up some way.

Then he said, "What Monique gonna do with your jeans? You 'bout a foot shorter than her."

Uh…

He said, "She was airbrushing them for you?"

I said, "Exactly."

He laughed. "Monique swear she Kimora Lee Simmons. Always designing something."

I laughed, too. "Right…"

"Go by her crib and get 'em."

I said, "We don't roll like that. I don't even know where she rests at." I decided to roll the dice. "I ain't living like the Huxtables…like Monique."

He said, "I heard that. I don't roll through her spot, either. I keep it straight hood."

"Exactly."

"I was really feeling that fatty, though."

"Give me Monique's address so I can get my jeans back and I'll really let you *feel* this fatty."

He said, "That's what's up," then proceeded to give me Monique's address. "Yo, I can get your math, though?"

"I got yours, I'll hit you back." Thank God I'd been smart enough to block my number before I called him.

"Mos def hit me back."

"Later."

I clicked off. I had everything I needed to track down Monique and get some answers.

There was only one way to find out the truth.

I was about to be up in Monique's hood like check-cashing spots and Chinese restaurants.

* * *

Except it wasn't a hood.

Homegirl was living like she'd written all those plays and movies instead of Tyler Perry. He came to mind because I was a mad black woman when I walked down Monique's street. Two buses and a hell of a walk later, I was finally there.

Of course her house was the last one on the expansive block. My feet were crying like Jerry Springer when he got the boot from *Dancing with the Stars*.

But I pressed on.

All the houses were beautiful. Manicured lawns, mailboxes with the family name engraved on them, luxury vehicles everywhere. It was like nothing I'd ever seen up close and personal. It made where I lived look like downtown Baghdad.

I couldn't help but dream of a fantasy life out here with Ricky.

Deep inside I knew that wasn't going to happen.

Michael Jackson would have a baby the old-fashioned way before that happened. I thought of Lark then. I needed my homegirl with me for moral support, but she was going through some family drama and I didn't want to pile my issues on the ones she already had. So Kenya was going for dolo. Alone. Solo.

Monique's house was the typical American dream. A two-story Colonial, complete with a white picket fence. It boasted a large open front porch and a beautiful flagstone walk you had to take to get to that porch. I was jealous and more than a little bit angry as I trotted down the walk.

I hadn't quite decided what I'd say when the door was answered.

I'd just have to freestyle.

Get my Kanye West on.

In one of my classes—I forget which class exactly—we talked about the three-second rule. Within three seconds of wanting to approach someone or a situation, we had to act or we'd succumb to doubt. I'd come too far for doubt. One way or another I was going to handle things that moment.

I rang the doorbell quickly.

A woman answered the door just as quickly.

I stood there, stunned by how beautiful she was.

More than three seconds passed.

She had almond-shaped eyes in a rich dark brown. Thick black hair, pulled back in a braid that kissed her butt. High cheekbones, pouty lips. A somewhat thin nose. Skin the color of pecan pie filling. Close to six feet tall.

And stylish to the nth.

She wore a cashmere turtleneck sweater that covered a graceful swan's neck. Dressed in all black, from her boots, to her hip-hugging jeans, to the cashmere sweater, of course.

She had a flat tummy, a healthy chest and strong thighs and legs that seemed to never end.

Maybe I had a little Sheryl Swoopes in me after all.

Nah.

I did want to be her when I grew up, though.

"Yes?" she asked. "May I help you?"

"I'm…I'm looking for Monique."

The corners of her mouth twitched, I noticed. "Monique's not in at the moment. Is there something I can help you with?"

"Do you know when she'll be in? I really need to speak with her."

"I didn't get your name, young lady."

I thought about what Monique had said at the Against All Odds store, about Ricky having my name scribbled all over his Beyoncé poster. I started to lie to that woman, in case Monique had mentioned my name to her. But I didn't lie. I was too in awe of her to lie. I didn't know if she was Monique's mother, but I suspected so. Monique was sure to turn from ugly duckling to swan if that was in fact her mother.

"My name's Kenya."

She said, "Are you one of Monique's classmates, Kenya?"

I shook my head. "No, I'm not."

"A friend?"

"No," I admitted. "More of a rival, I suppose."

Surprise found her face. "Rival? Over what?"

I said, "A boy."

She frowned. The good cheer left her face. "Come inside, Kenya."

I hesitated.

"I don't bite," she said, in a tone that let me know it was a lie. She definitely bit if need be.

We moved inside, through a spotless foyer to an equally spotless living room. The television was playing, on some cooking show. She turned the sound down with a universal remote, tossed the remote on a chair and extended her arm toward one of the suede couches in the room. "Sit."

That was a command.

I sat.

She did, as well. On the couch I hadn't chosen.

She said, "Tell me about this boy."

I asked, "Are you Monique's mom?"

She frowned again and then nodded. "Tell me about this boy."

"He's my boyfriend now. But before me he was with Monique."

I noticed her jaw tense. Intense interest was on her face. "Really, now?"

"Monique didn't talk about her boyfriend?"

"I'm just her mother," she said. "Last to know."

"I'm sorry."

"Never knew Monique even had any interest in boys. She was awkward, self-conscious."

I said, "Was?"

She tried to fight something off but couldn't. Tears filled her eyes. She fanned in front of her face, tried her best to chase down some composure. I didn't see her as the type of woman who broke down often. But this was an emotional meeting for her. I kept a small pack of Kleenex in my purse; I pulled out the pack and handed several to Monique's mom. She blotted her eyes, blew her nose. After a while she sighed, smiled.

She said, "I apologize for that."

"It's okay." I hesitated. "Is Monique all right?"

She looked at me with a sadness I've only seen on one woman's face ever before: my mama's the day my daddy left for good.

She said, "I'll be right back. I want to show you something."

I looked around while she was gone. Her CD tower was pretty one-dimensional: all jazz CDs. A bookshelf was stuffed with mostly academic texts: medical books and investing tomes. Black African sculptures were carefully appointed throughout the room. Paintings were on the walls. If Mama had had this woman's money, our house would have looked the same. Mama had a penchant for Afrocentric sculptures and whatnot, too. This place was especially beautiful; made me want to go out and purchase some art myself. I'd never been in a house that made me so proud to be black.

I went up to a particularly beautiful picture, touched its edges with my fingertips. The surface wasn't smooth. It was an authentic painting.

"Women's work is never done," I heard from behind me. I turned. "I'm sorry?"

"That painting you were looking at. That's what it's called. *Women's Work Is Never Done*. It's by Sadie Patterson."

"It's beautiful."

"That it is, Kenya."

Suddenly, I was embarrassed. "I don't even know Monique's last name. I'd like to address you respectfully, Mrs…?"

"Ms.," she corrected me gently. "Monique's father and I divorced when she was a little girl. Done it all by my lonesome. For the most part it's been more rewarding than difficult. Raising a girl can be tough, and a black girl, at that. I thank God for His grace in my situation." She was so unlike my own mother. No bitterness lived inside her. It was refreshing to get that perspective.

I looked over toward her bookshelf. "You're a nurse?"

"Doctor, obstetrics." She smiled gently. Everything about the woman was graceful. An odd emotion captured me; shamed me, too. I wished she were my mother. "But to answer your question, Kenya, our last name is Thompson. But I don't like formal. Makes me feel old. Just call me Scent."

"Scent?"

She smiled again and moved into the room. "Well, it's Millicent, actually, but Scent has kind of stuck. Thank God for small miracles."

I liked her a lot.

I said, "I'm sorry I came over here like this. I don't know what I was thinking, what I was hoping to accomplish."

Scent said, "We'll get to that, Kenya. I want to show you these things. Sit."

That time the word—sit—was spoken with warmth.

I sat.

She did, too. On the couch, right next to me.

In her hands were two shoe boxes. You had to be Italian to read the names on the boxes. She had expensive tastes to go along with everything else, I realized.

Boy, did I want to be like her when I grew up.

Scent opened one of the boxes and handed me a leather-bound photo album. I opened it to pages and pages of a small, awkward-looking girl. She was skinny, tall for her age, with glasses too big for her head and teeth too big for her mouth. I thought of Lark.

"She's a two, Ken."

"Too skinny."

"Teeth too big."

I said, "Monique."

Scent surprised me, said, "No. Me."

"You?" I was dumbfounded. "Couldn't be. You're beautiful."

"Thank you, Kenya." She paused, gathered her thoughts. "I'd like to think I was beautiful then, too. And that my daughter is now. I was awkward, for sure...just like Monique. But there was a beauty in my awkwardness. There's beauty in hers."

I didn't cosign that thought.

She said, "Black girls...black women...we have it

tough. Society doesn't celebrate our beauty, our natural beauty. Too many of us walking around believing we have to go to the extremes of Lil' Kim to be beautiful."

I said, "I think Lil' Kim looks a hot mess now. She took plastic surgery to a whole 'nother level."

Scent nodded, tapped one of her old photos. "That beautiful little awkward girl that grew into a beautiful woman would have given her eyeteeth to look like Lil' Kim. Toni Morrison's novel pretty much sums up how I felt about myself."

I said, "You're talking about *The Bluest Eye?*"

Scent smiled. "You know the book?"

"I do."

The corners of her mouth twitched again. "Gave it to Monique years ago, a birthday gift. She read it, but it didn't affect her in the way I hoped."

I took the mention of Monique as a chance to redirect the conversation.

"Is Monique all right?"

Scent looked at me. "Are you sexually active with this boy, Kenya? Monique's old boyfriend."

I shook my head. "No. I'm a virgin." And I don't know what came over me but I added, "Close, though. I mean… if everything were everything…I would."

Scent touched my hands. "Hold on to your gift, Kenya."

"My gift?"

"Your body and who you offer it to is a precious gift, Kenya. That decision shouldn't be made lightly. It's like a beautiful flower, Kenya. We must start thinking of it that way. That's why they call it deflowering a woman, I want to say. It's a beautiful flower, Kenya. I tried to get that message across to..." She couldn't finish the thought.

I gulped. "My boyfriend was with your daughter?"

"Trampled my baby's rose garden." The bitterness that lived in my mama was in Scent's tone for the first time.

I thought about my next question for what felt like an eternity before I worked up the courage to ask, "Is Monique pregnant?"

Scent swallowed. "What have you heard?"

"That she's pregnant and you shipped her down south to have the baby."

Scent closed her eyes, breathed deeply. "We live in a YouTube, MySpace, and TMZ.com world. I guess there are no secrets anymore. People can't even live their lives without intrusion."

I took that moment to close my eyes. Breathe deeply my own self. I hadn't wanted it to be true. I wanted my boyfriend to be special. I wanted to be special.

Scent asked, "What's his name, Kenya?"

I opened my eyes. Didn't even hesitate. "Ricky. Ricky Williams."

"I'd like to speak to this young man."

I pulled out my cell phone, dialed Ricky's number. He didn't answer. That was the way it had been the past few days. I kept dialing the number back. More than ten times in a row. Finally, he picked up. The anger in his voice startled me. I handed the phone to Scent. I stood up then and went back to the Sadie Patterson painting. *Women's Work Is Never Done*. Again, I touched it.

I heard Scent say, "I've been looking forward to having a word with you, young man."

Eric

This should be easy.

But it's difficult.

I have the card with Fiasco's number on it in my left hand.

I have a cordless phone in my other hand.

All I have to do is dial.

I am ten dialed digits away from hanging with someone most people could only come in contact with through BET or MTV. I imagine how the kids at school would treat me if they knew I was best buddies with Fiasco. The snickers would stop. The taunts would cease. Guys would want to shoot hoops with me. Girls would invite me over when their parents weren't home, and not so I could help them memorize all the presidents, either.

I place the phone back in the cradle.

I'm just Eric Posey. I'm not cool. I never will be. I need to put aside this fantasy.

The phone rings. I don't even have to look at the caller

ID. Only one person ever calls me. I hesitate. Contemplate answering the call. But I don't. On the fourth ring the tape from my old-fashioned answering machine clicks on.

Benny starts out slow.

"Hey, Eric."

There's about fifteen seconds of white noise before his voice comes on again.

"Being friends means never having to say you're sorry." He sniffs out a self-conscious laugh. "I got that from a Hallmark card. Pretty cool, huh?"

I look at Fiasco's card. It's still in my hand.

"But I am sorry, Eric. I'm very sorry. I can't tell you enough. My dad was very upset, too. He's color-blind. And so am I. You're my best friend. I thought we'd always be. I can't imagine it otherwise. I keep calling and leaving you these messages. I don't mind. We're friends. But…well, give me a call back. Please."

At some point I have to start thinking selfishly. Or else I will commit myself to a life of unpopularity. Benny's been a good friend, for sure. But he's the wrong friend. No question about it, the kids at school view me as the lame black kid with the lame white boy as a best friend. That doesn't win me any points. Benny prevents me from ever getting in the inner circle.

Fiasco, on the other hand, offers nothing but hope.

When Benny's voice fades away and the tape stops re-cording, I pick up the phone and dial Fiasco's ten digits.

I have a feeling my life will never be the same again.

* * *

Twenty minutes later, I'm standing on the curb in front of our place, waiting patiently. My wait isn't long. A black Range Rover pulls up, idles, its windows rattling with the loud sounds of one of Fiasco's earliest songs. I know the words verbatim. I move toward the vehicle. And wait.

And wait.

And wait.

Finally, the passenger-side window slides down.

I expect to see Fiasco, but a woman is in the driver's seat.

"You gonna stand there all night?" she asks.

She looks like one of the girls in the Pussycat Dolls. Exotic and beautiful. It's hard for me to get my thoughts together. My brain doesn't want to send the directive to my legs to move. *Nicole Scherzinger,* I keep thinking. *Lead girl in the Dolls, has a video out now with T.I. Could it be?*

"Get in, boy," she says.

I get in.

I say, "Hi."

"High is right. You were standing out there like you smoked something today."

"Sorry about that. Wasn't sure what to do."

She nods at me, says, "My name's Mya."

That disappoints me, briefly. I wanted her to be Nicole Scherzinger. Wanted to be cool with two celebrities. On the job one day and already I'm greedy. But even though she isn't a Pussycat Doll, I'm okay. She's too beautiful for me to stay disappointed for long.

I say, "I'm Eric."

"I know."

"Where's Fiasco?"

"I'll take you to him."

We ride in silence for a while, and then I say, "You look like the girl in the Pussycat Dolls."

She nods. "I get that a lot. Her and Kim Kardashian."

"You're..."

"Beautiful, I know, but thanks."

I wish I had that kind of confidence. Wish I could say the things she says so effortlessly. Swagger. It's refreshing. She has it in abundance. Fiasco has it, too. So many of the boys and girls at my school are blessed with it, Kenya among them. So it's in my bloodlines. It's just dormant. That's it. Well, I'm going to pull it out.

I look at Mya, say, "I could see myself Windexing your pants."

She frowns. "What nonsense are you talking?"

"I meant," I say, "I'd like to put Windex down your pants."

"I'm a second away from dropping you off on the side of the road somewhere," she says, shakes her head and adds, "Fiasco and his crazy ideas."

All the cylinders aren't quite clicking. I heard the line once. Thought it was cute, that girls would adore it. Until now I haven't found one to use it on. And now that I have, I can't quite get it together. Windex. Windex. Windex. *Think, Eric. Think. Think. Think.*

Oh.

I say, "Did you wash your pants with Windex?"

Mya just looks at me. I'm not prepared for that.

"'C-c-cause," I stutter, determined to see this through, "girl, I can see myself in them."

She only says two words in response. "Don't speak."

I don't for the rest of the ride.

Mya pulls the car off the main road, into a motel complex. The motel offers nightly and hourly rates, and my best guess is the hour-at-a-time customers far outnumber those staying for the entire night. Just off a main avenue, hidden behind a mini shopping plaza, its neighbors out front are a flower nursery, a sporting goods shop and a dry cleaner. All of the businesses are Korean-owned, except for the motel, according to Mya. "A gang of Patels run the place," she says.

"What?"

"Patels," she repeats. "Indians."

"Oh."

Floodlights spread throughout the courtyard cast an ominous orange glow. I should be home in my room, or at best, over at Benny's house trying to figure out Halo 3. Large green bushes, cousins of some stubborn weed, dot the yard. Tan garden gravel crackles under our tires as Mya drives the Range Rover up to the building and parks it.

"Fiasco's here?" I ask.

"You'll have to wait and see."

She doesn't say any more than that.

I shouldn't be here.

Mya cuts the engine, opens her door and steps out. I follow suit.

A lowrider late-model sports car idles in a spot by the office. Loud music rattles its windows. Not Fiasco, though. Tupac. The car's windows are black with tint, but nowhere near as dark as the Range Rover's. Its original paint is sanded away, leaving what looks like a terra-cotta pottery project, a clay-orange finish. Platinum rims are on its wheels; the wheels beneath the rims are painted in a rich bloodred.

I think: *Gang.*

Bloods.

"What are we going to do here?" I ask Mya.

"You'll have to wait and see," is all she says.

The driver's-side door of the lowrider blows open as Mya and I approach the building. A young black male with his hair styled in cornrows, a silky-looking football jersey hanging from his lanky frame, hops out. His features are canine, sharp. Skin holds a medium-brown coloring, hair carries a serious sheen. His eyes are dead. He puts me in mind of a Doberman.

I don't like dogs. They've been known to bite me, or, at the very least, growl at me hard.

Two more young black males move from the lowrider, as well. All of them are tall and in football jerseys, all with dead eyes. Deader even than Crash's that day he nearly beat the life out of me. Not a care in the world; that's the message delivered by their dead eyes. I understand immediately what that means. Trouble. Possibly lots of it.

I slow down, but Mya keeps moving with her not-a-care-in-the-world strut. It's the strut of the beautiful girl walking through the club in any rapper's video, or the girl who's just stepped dripping wet from the pool and knows with a certainty how much lovelier all her curves look with water raining from them. I keep moving, too, but slowly, tentatively. I want to turn around, but I can't do that, either.

Someone cuts the engine on the lowrider. Tupac vanishes into the ether.

Doberman says to Mya, "*Dayum*, girl. You fine as frog hair. Come holla at a player."

Mya stops then. Moths dance against the motel building. With the coolness of the night air, the orange glow from the floodlights and these three thugs in our path, it's starting to feel like a modern-day Western. I'm not John Wayne by any stretch of the imagination. I'm not even John Starks, the gunslinger who used to shoot basketballs for the New York Knicks when I was a little bitty boy. Back before my father left. I remember sitting on his lap watching games. Wonder how he'd feel if he saw me now. Wonder how I'd feel.

Oh, well.

Doberman says, "Yo. You heard me talking to you, girl?"

He moves from the cover of the lowrider's door, positions himself on the sidewalk in front of the car. The two others follow suit, stand before me and Mya and block our path. A standoff is definitely taking place. I want to run for my life. But like I said, I can't. I don't know what is keeping me here.

I say, "We don't want any trouble."

Doberman says, "You better school homegirl here, then. Tell her to speak when spoken to."

I tell Mya, "It *is* rude to ignore a person's greeting."

She turns and looks at me with disgust. Does that nose-wrinkle thing. "Are you serious?"

Then she turns back to the three of them. "Y'all need to stop playing thug and get out of our way."

Doberman says, "You need to chill with talking greasy just because you got Steve Urkel here watching your back." He laughs.

I say, "Why do I have to always be Steve Urkel?"

They all ignore me.

"And," Doberman says, "we ain't hardly playing thug."

He lifts his jersey, a Detroit Lions throwback Barry Sanders. My gaze drifts to the waistband of his baggy pants. I can't believe my eyes. What I see is something I've only witnessed in Bruce Willis or Will Smith action movies. This is way too much. "Sounds like thunder it goes off," Doberman boasts. "My boys are holding, too."

I home in on the other two. One is adorned in Art Monk's Redskins jersey, the other in Lawrence Taylor's Giants jersey. Numbers eighty-one and fifty-six respectively. This is way more serious than my confrontation with Crash outside school, but it places me in mind of that moment. I expect Benny to tap my shoulder at any moment, wake me up from this nightmare.

All I wanted was to be cool.

I can't say that desire is worth all of this trouble, though.

Mya says, "Listen, Snoopy, why don't you guys get back in your flowerpot and leave before this thing turns ugly."

Doberman says, "You dissing my whip?"

"And *you,* Snoopy," Mya adds.

Now, I've had so many moments where someone has said something demeaning and humiliating to me. My head always swims with quick comebacks and snappy responses I could say in retaliation. I never do, though. I almost always have kept my mouth shut. That's the safe bet. I believe in safe bets.

I do admire Mya's courage, though.

Just not tonight. And just not with these three.

Did she not see what was tucked so snug in the waistband of Doberman's pants?

So I say, "She didn't mean that," to ease the tension.

"Yes I did, Eric," she barks at me. "Every last word of it. And I have more."

I say, "No, you didn't mean it. And you certainly don't have more."

She says, "Yes I did. And I do. I was going to say something about his two boys being fleas."

"Hey," Doberman yells. "Y'all need to be concerned with me, not each other."

I say, "You're right, Doberman. We're sorry."

He says, "What did you call me, Urkel?"

Mya laughs. "He called your dog-looking ass a Doberman."

Did I?

Whoops. Didn't realize I'd vocalized what was floating around in my head. Big mistake.

Doberman takes a step in my direction, says, "See now…"

Just then a song plays. Usher. Doberman looks down, frowns. He says, "Dayum," and pulls his jersey up again, yanks a cell phone from his belt clip. Backs away. "Speak."

Doberman's two homies continue to block our path.

Mya says, "What you two got?"

Art Monk ice grills her. "What's that, bird?"

She nods toward his belt line. "What you got as your cell phone ringtone? Ciara? Mariah Carey? Some ol' hard gully stuff…Mary J. Blige?"

"I know you ain't clownin' nobody, bird."

Mya continues, "John Legend. India.Arie."

"Yo, bird…"

Mya is relentless. "Alicia Keys. Chris Brown. Ne-Yo."

Art Monk looks over at Lawrence Taylor as Mya keeps naming R & B crooners. She will not shut up. Art Monk and Lawrence Taylor have no idea how to handle her. I don't know how to handle her, either. You have to treat her like a storm, let her run her course and hope and pray that she doesn't inflict too much damage.

"J. Holiday. Trey Songz. Brian McKnight…" she continues.

Doberman reappears, a bounce in his step. "We out," he says to Monk and LT.

"What?" they say in unison. Confusion is thick in their tones; so is disappointment.

"Got something else to do," Doberman says. "That takes precedence over this nonsense."

Mya says, "*Precedence.* Now I know you ain't a thug. You're probably matriculated at Princeton."

Doberman says, "I don't go to no Princeton."

Mya smiles. "Didn't even ask what *matriculated* means. See that?"

Doberman opens his mouth. Whatever thought was there doesn't come out. He waves her off and moves away. Monk and LT follow. They get back in the lowrider. The engine rumbles to life. Tupac's gravelly voice awakens. Doberman pulls off, spewing tan garden gravel as he peels out of the motel complex.

Mya says, "Wannabes." Then she looks at me and smiles. "Doberman, huh? I liked that, baby boy. You're tougher than I thought. For a minute there I thought you were gonna be a punk."

I've been elevated in her mind. "*Baby boy,*" she called me. I love that, so I don't bother letting her know the Doberman comment was a slip of the tongue. I say, "I go for mines, girl."

Something I've heard Crash say.

Mya pinches my cheek. "If you were three years older... oomph."

I guess the Windex flub is forgiven. I feel rejuvenated, refreshed.

I say, "In three years I will be."

She laughs. "Come on, Fiasco's waiting."

"Thought you said he wasn't here."

She smiles. "Never said that. Told you you'd have to wait and see. You'll see what I mean soon enough."

He's holed up in one of the rooms.

Mya knocks at the door. Two quick knocks, pause, three quick knocks. I take it to be some kind of code. The door cracks open. Then the chain lock is removed. Mya walks in. I follow.

Fiasco's dressed down in a terry-cloth robe and house slippers. He smiles and nods when he sees me. "What's good, son?"

Mya says, "We had a little trouble outside. Wannabe thugs. Eric handled it."

"Eric did?"

"Yep."

Fiasco comes over, gives me dap. "That's what I'm talking about."

I say, "You know how I do."

Something I've heard Crash say.

I look around the room. It's the opposite of elegant. Wallpaper is peeling; an intense odor of roach spray is in the air, which doesn't seem to deter the roach I notice scurrying up the wall. A desk in one corner of the room has a scented candle burning on it; a thick phone book keeps it from toppling over. The chair by the desk has a ripped cushion; foam bleeds out of the rip. The curtains are a nice pink. Nothing else in the room is pink. Or goes with pink, for that matter.

I say, "Nice place."

Fiasco says, "It's garbage. But I have to get in this element to do what I'm going to do."

I don't like the sound of that. "What are you going to do?"

Mya says, "This is the part I was referring to, Eric."

Fiasco frowns, nods toward the desk. I move over there. There's a notepad on the surface, several pens, words scribbled all over the notepad. "I write rhymes, Eric. I'm working on a new album. But it isn't going to be a Fiasco album."

I laugh away my anxiety and look at the notepad. Notice a couple lines:

> *I let off rounds*
> *No MC's better*
> *My skin's made of platinum*
> *I don't sweat or stick to leather*
> *A murder MC*
> *Squeeze off till da Glock is empty*

Mya says, "I'm taking a shower," and walks off. She stops at the bathroom door. "You did well, baby boy." Then she's gone.

I say, "She's a sweet lady."

Fiasco says, "Had her in every single one of my videos. Mya changes looks for each one, so people don't even realize it's the same girl. We're like Spike Lee and Denzel... we get together and magic just seems to happen. And Mya isn't your typical video girl. She's more ambitious and motivated than anyone I know. She puts Karrine Steffans to shame."

I say, "Superhead."

Fiasco looks at me, frowns. "What you know about that?"

"*Confessions of a Video Vixen.* I read the book."

He shakes his head. "They really need to put parental advisory stickers on books, too."

I joke, "You're not Papa, are you?"

Papa is an infamous person from the book. The only celebrity Karrine Steffans didn't mention by real name. Google *Papa and Superhead* and you'll get close to a million hits.

Fiasco says, "Nah, son. I'm not Papa."

I nod at the notepad. "What did you mean before? About this not being a Fiasco album."

"I've catered to the women 'cause they buy the records," he says. "My stuff has an edge, but not enough. I don't have street credibility right now. So I'm gullying myself up a bit...putting out a record under my alter ego's name."

"Which is?"

"Murdaa. But spelled with two *A*'s at the end instead of *E-R*."

I say, "Catchy."

He nods. "Yeah."

I say, "So why the reinvention?"

"It's getting harder and harder to move units. I needed to try something different."

I say, "Murdaa...with two *A*'s at the end instead of *E-R?*"

"Exactly."

"You're gonna be talking guns and killing?"

"I'm gonna spit my reality."

"You're rich," I remind him. "You probably live in a gated community. Guns and killing is hardly your reality."

"I'm comfortable," he replies. "But I came from the gutter. I was born in Camden, son. Moms got us up out of the murder capital of Jersey as quick as she could. We ended up moving up north. East Orange, Newark, Irvington. Lot of bouncing around. The only constant was we'd be in a hood. I lost three friends before I graduated high school. All of 'em shot dead."

I say, "So with all that negative experience you want to pump tales of guns and killing into the community?"

"I want to entertain and educate, Reverend Al." He smiles at the Reverend Al Sharpton comment. I'm far from Sharpton. Just concerned about the music. It's all guns and violence from all the rappers. Very few are able to buck the trend, are comfortable enough to go against the grain. Fiasco happening to be one of them.

I say, "I take it you won't be having a song with Kelly Rowland on this album?"

He frowns. "That was a top-ten hit. I stacked a lot of paper off the ringtone alone. But I lost millions in respect. I have to get that back by any means necessary. So, to answer your question, no, Kelly Rowland won't be on this album. I won't be doing anything resembling that anytime soon."

I say, "Why not? Those pop songs have worked for everyone from LL Cool J to Nelly."

"No disrespect to either of them, but the streets ain't checking for them."

"The streets don't make rappers go platinum," I remind him.

He nods. "True enough. But…I want my street cred. It's important to me. I will still do the Fiasco stuff. Matter fact, I'm just about finished with a new Fiasco album. Ready to shoot the video, which you'll be in, if everything is everything. But this project is near and dear to my heart. This is just a little creative departure."

"How do you bounce from Fiasco to Murdaa and not have folks question which one is the real you? Seems like that'll cause confusion. The street cats aren't going to respect you as hard."

He stops me with an upraised hand. "You're making my head spin. Enough of this talk. I've got something I want to give you."

He steps away from me and heads for the desk. Opens the drawer. Pauses with his back to me, as if contemplating something. Then he turns back to me. In his hands I notice the Dirty Jersey medallion and chain he's famous for wearing. He moves over to me, medallion and chain still in his hands. "I appreciate you playing devil's advocate. You're good for me, E.P. You'll keep me honest. Having you around is good."

Then he says one word. It's the best word I've ever heard. One I've always sought, seldom found.

"Welcome."

I look at the building. It's a one-story structure, concrete painted white, with concertina wire around the entire perimeter. It looks and feels like a place where you would come to purchase a John Deere riding lawn mower. It isn't, though. It's ominous in the same way the motel complex was. My gut tells me to end this now, stop chasing the elusive dream of being popular, and somehow find my way back home.

I feel for my neck. Run my fingers over the thick chain and medallion Fiasco placed over my head not even an hour ago. He'd told me then that I'd get the Dirty Jersey tattoo, as well, if I wanted it, and that a select few have the chain, and even fewer can boast of the chain and the tattoo. I'm special, that means.

There is no turning back for me.

A caravan of more black SUVs pull into the lot. Escalades, Expeditions, Range and Land Rovers, a couple Hummers. All the vehicles are black, all with the darkest tint possible on their windows. Various songs, played at ear-drum-shattering levels, compete with one another from the SUVs' stereo speakers. Young people file out of the cars, their excitement palpable. Fiasco has drivers for each vehicle. They exit, as well. Dudes he grew up with, he told me on the ride over. Tough cats, every single one of them. And they're large. All business. Like the men who guard Minister Louis Farrakhan. Fruit of Islam, I believe they are called. Each one has the Dirty Jersey medallion, the tattoo. I'm the only member of Fiasco's clique that didn't grow up with him in Camden.

All the young people who file from the SUVs are dressed in some form of hip-hop gear.

All of them are cool. With that swagger Fiasco always talks about.

And I'm among them, but better than them. I have the medallion.

Staccato popping sounds burst out and interrupt my reverie. Sounds like the gunfire you're apt to hear at Crash's building in the projects.

I should leave.

I look over toward the SUVs. Fiasco emerges from Mya's black Range Rover after the young people have gone inside. He looks the Range Rover over appreciatively for a brief moment and then makes his way in my direction. The Range Rover's engine comes to life. Then the truck pulls away, Mya at the wheel. Fiasco stops beside me. It's just me and him. A party of two. Again, I'm special.

I say, "Where's Mya going?"

"She doesn't like it here. It's best she keeps it moving. I don't press the issue."

I ask, "That gunfire I hear? Sounds like gunfire."

Fiasco says, "Got this place dirt cheap. Me and my homies...shorties, too...and I'm talking video-ho fine... come out here and convalesce. R and R, ya heard?"

He didn't answer my question about the gunfire. I don't repeat it.

I say, "You bought this place just to have a place to chill?"

He nods. "And do business. I ain't shortsighted. I hustle hard out of here."

My mind flashes to the movie *Belly,* a vehicle to showcase the acting skills of rappers Nas, DMX and others. My mind also flashes on *New Jack City*. Gangsta flicks. Women, in bras and panties, at some out-of-the-place spot similar to this one Fiasco has brought me to, packaging drugs for sale. Hustling hard.

Fiasco must notice something shift in me, because he puts his hand on my shoulder and says, "Nothing illegal, son. I'm like Fif now. Still on my grind, still on the hustle, get rich or die trying and all that, but always through legal enterprise. Jail ain't a good look. I understand that." He stops, smiles. "Even though I gotta admit a minute on lockdown wouldn't hurt my album sales. Jail is a marketing campaign for rappers. Who needs an ad in *Vibe;* just one day in the clink beats that." He laughs at that last part. I do, too. Even though my mother has always taught me that jail is not a laughing matter.

More of what sounds like gunfire pierces the air. I ignore it.

I ask Fiasco, "So what kind of hustle do you do out of here, then?"

His eyes light up. "I'm glad you asked. T-shirts. Removable Dirty Jersey tattoo strips. Mass-produce all of them mix-tape CDs I be putting out. Sell them shits for ten dollars a pop. This place is one big assembly line, son."

I nod. "You put out more mix tapes than Lil' Wayne and Game combined."

"Hustlin'."

More SUVs arrive. A cluster of more young people pass by. Fiasco stops and gives a dap to every one of them. But they all move past. His time is with me and me alone. I am moved by that, because contained in that cluster were two girls with more goods than Buffie the Body or any of the girls featured in *XXL* magazine's "Eye Candy" spread.

Fiasco says, "Why don't we step inside. I'll show you the place."

I follow, bopping with the finesse of Crash as I walk.

For some reason my awkwardness is dissolving with every second I spend in Fiasco's presence. By the end of the day I'll be ready to scoop up some fine young honey and beat down even the toughest dude in the bunch. Maybe.

Two supersized black dudes are just inside. They stand by a counter like one you would find in a store. One is in tight blue jeans, combat boots that aren't Timberlands, and a black leather Fonz jacket that runs about two sizes too small for his enormous upper body. He looks to be in his mid- to late forties, but he's in incredible shape. The other is younger, closer to Fiasco's age, and is an obvious New York Jets fan. He has a wide nose, long dreadlocks that hang from under a green and white Jets cap to kiss the collar of a green and white Jets jacket. Like the black Fonz wannabe, he's also in tight blue jeans and a pair of stomping boots. Nothing hip-hop about either of them.

But both of them are the size of a small continent.

I ask Fiasco, "Everybody you know have to shop for their clothes at the big 'n' tall store?"

He laughs, nods. "Yup. My homies from around the way. The biggest and the baddest. I made sure of that."

Fiasco shakes both of their hands. No dap. A handshake. "Holding down the fort?" he asks.

The Black Fonz says, "On it like white on rice."

I'm new to this cool thing, every interaction is a lesson, and yet even I know not to ever repeat that phrase around anyone with swagger. I blame it on his age.

Mr. Jets adds, "I saw your wifey pull out of the lot. She ever gonna step a foot inside this place? I'm feeling put off, like I must have leprosy or something."

Fiasco looks at the Black Fonz, frowns. "You had me until that wifey part. I started drowning you out then. I am single and enjoying it. Don't ever get that twisted."

Mr. Jets says, "Enjoying it, that's an understatement."

Fiasco smiles. Mr. Jets smiles, too. The Black Fonz is noticeably quiet and unemotional.

Mr. Jets says, "I think I'd settle down, though, if I had a female of Mya's caliber sniffing my tail."

Fiasco nods. "Mya's fine. But she's high maintenance. Difficult to satisfy. You really knew her, you wouldn't want to be bothered. The girl has issues." He looks at the Black Fonz. And, of course, the Black Fonz remains unemotional.

Mr. Jets asks, "How you figure?"

Fiasco says, "It is what it is. Like this Cuban girl I dealt with once. Making love to her was work. She was so proud of being a Latina, and you know she hated hip-hop, so I tried to be smart, got some Celia Cruz CDs to listen to while I tapped that Goya-bean booty."

"So what happened?"

"No go. She couldn't stand Celia Cruz. She liked Luther."

The two of them laugh. The Black Fonz doesn't even crack a smile. I wonder what's wrong with the guy.

The laughter breaks. Fiasco says, "Mya's like that. Difficult to please."

Mr. Jets pulls on the back of his jacket, fidgets just a bit, and then says, "So tell us what song gets Mya in the mood?"

"For me to know and you to *never* find out," Fiasco says. The frown on his face is clear. He's not happy with the question.

The Black Fonz finally speaks. "You gonna let this guy keep salivating over your precious Mya, *Fiasco?*" He says Fiasco's name like it's an insult, like it's a dirty word.

Mr. Jets puts his hands up. "I wouldn't take it there. I was just saying."

The Black Fonz says, "You were just saying quite a bit. If I was *Fiasco,* I'd knock out your fronts." The Black Fonz eyeballs Fiasco like they have major beef. Fiasco eyeballs him back with the same intensity.

Seconds tick by without a response from either of them. They both assume the stance of bulls ready to run over anything in their way. I can feel the tension in the air. It's as thick as Melyssa Ford, one of the video vixens plastered on my bedroom wall. That is quite thick, let me tell you.

"Mya can handle herself," Fiasco says after some time.

"She's good peoples," Mr. Jets agrees.

Fiasco nods. "No doubt." His gaze falls on the Black Fonz.

The Black Fonz says, "Seen her drive outta here like she was running from something."

Fiasco moves over to him, claps him on the shoulder. "Enough of Mya, okay?"

The Black Fonz stares at him for a moment and then nods.

Nothing more is said regarding Mya.

Fiasco turns to me. "What do you think of the place?"

I nod my approval.

The building is an old warehouse. It's huge. My mind travels further into the bowels of the place. What could be in here that Mya dislikes so much?

Fiasco says, "My bad. Trent, Alonzo, this here is my lil' homie, E.P."

E.P.

My initials.

I like that.

Trent and Alonzo both shake my hand. Or, I should say, their hands swallow mine. I've been known to describe someone with large hands as having hands like baseball mitts. Crash has hands like that. That description wouldn't fit Trent or Alonzo, though. Their hands are bigger than that. A whole lot bigger.

Trent says, "Here to get corrupted?" Trent is Mr. Jets.

Alonzo adds, "Another one bites the dust." Alonzo is the Black Fonz, of course.

Fiasco shoos them off, says, "Don't listen to these two country-western Negroes. Come fly with me, E.P."

He moves away.

I nod at the two giants, follow Fiasco.

It isn't long before I know exactly what that sound is I've been hearing. The one that sounds like gunfire.

It's gunfire.

A large area is sectioned off as a shooting range. It's packed with people laughing, smiling and dancing to the music blaring from mounted speakers. Doing everything but paying extra care to the guns they have in hand.

Fiasco says, "Point one on the syllabus for Hustlin' 101. I charge these fools twenty bucks and they get ammunition, a firearm and a pack of five paper targets to take out their aggression on."

I say, "There are an awful lot of them."

A thought nudges at my mind. Feels like Fiasco is a rap

Al Qaeda, training Bloods and Crips to destroy our community in the same way Osama bin Laden had his folks attack our buildings, our sense of safety, our very lives.

I nudge that thought away.

Fiasco says, "Economics lesson. Count heads and multiply that number by twenty. It's the most beautifullest thing in the world."

I say, "Stop biting Keith Murray."

"Forgot you were a hip-hop historian." Fiasco smiles. "I loved that song."

"Heard the new one he's got with Tyrese?"

Fiasco shakes his head. His mind isn't on songs, rap comebacks, anything to do with the music. He motions with his head to another counter area by the shooting range. I look over.

There's an NRA poster on the wall behind the counter, a large sign next to it with house rules for the shooting range. *LOAD and HANDLE firearms ONLY WHEN YOU ARE READY TO SHOOT THEM. SIGHT and HEARING PROTECTION must be worn at ALL TIMES in the range area. The call "CEASE FIRE" or the sound of a WHISTLE means STOP SHOOTING IMMEDIATELY AND STEP AWAY FROM THE SHOOTING AREA.*

Fiasco says, "Media paints us rappers as common criminals. I'm trying to educate my young people, make 'em more responsible in everything they do. They gonna pick up guns anyway...."

What Fiasco really wants me to believe, I think, is that Murdaa is actually going to be a socially conscious rapper.

I want to tell Fiasco that the young boy doing Soulja Boy's dance with a firearm in his hand is breaking most of the shooting range rules. But I don't.

Fiasco says, "Shooting stalls are ten yards long. Climate controlled, too. Have exhaust systems. Got every kind of pistol you can think of. Calibers run from .22 to AE50."

I nod with a blank look in my eyes. The closest I've ever come in contact with gun talk is watching episodes of *The Wire* on HBO or listening to rap CDs. Crash is more evolved when it comes to guns. I don't want to be evolved that way myself. I want no part of guns. I can't see myself among those using the shooting range.

Fiasco continues, "This is a business. I'm an entity, I'm a business, hustlin' like Fif, grindin' until I get rich or die trying, trying to make a better way for myself and all the little shorties that come up like I did. This ain't no BS spot, E.P. This much bigger than that, ya heard? Like Jay-Z said, 'I'm a businessman.'"

I nod at his little speech.

Fiasco says, "You feelin' me, E.P.? You understand where I'm coming from?"

"Yes."

Off in another corner of the warehouse, a group of Fiasco's Dirty Jersey boys are crowded around the two girls from earlier, the "Eye Candy" dimepieces who walked in after we arrived. Despite the girls' curves, I realize they're young. It's in their faces, in their eyes. Wide-eyed innocence they call it. Too young for the Dirty Jersey boys, yet some serious romancing is taking place. I feel uncomfortable watching it transpire. Then Mr. Jets and the Black Fonz arrive on the scene. *Good,* I think. They'll clean it up, keep it PG-13. To my surprise, something else happens. The two girls drift off through a door marked PRIVATE with the Black Fonz on their heels. Mr. Jets stands guard over the door like the president's Secret Service detail.

I try to shake the image of the Black Fonz's hands on the young girls' butts as he ushered them into the PRIVATE room.

Fiasco claps me on the shoulder, changes my focus.

He says, "So, seriously, you wanna really be down with Dirty Jersey, son? I'm willing to seriously put you on. Let you deep in the fold. And I don't do that for everyone. Usually it takes a long time before I offer that respect to anyone. I'm not one for quick ascension. You gotta earn your stripes in my camp. But you, E.P., you have already. I don't know what it is. Maybe that you remind me of myself. Anyway, you wanna be put on?"

I look around the warehouse. Gunfire and excited voices are the sound track. Murdaa music. I look at the door marked PRIVATE. Unthinkable things could be happening in there. Most likely *are* happening in there. Two girls my age or close to it. Is that something I'd want to get down with? Can my conscience pretend that part of the Dirty Jersey situation doesn't exist?

The flip side?

I'd be part of a very select crowd. I'd be special. The cool boys and girls would envy me.

I look at Fiasco. "Yes. I want to be put on with your crew."

I don't think another thought about the two young girls in that PRIVATE room with the Black Fonz.

sister

Vera was dead on her feet, in a pair of turned-over Reeboks with filthy shoelaces. Best she could afford on her meager waitress wages. She had other expenses that were more important than the sneakers, like the rent and electricity, and so she sacrificed with her footwear. She was thin from all the time standing and getting very little food in her belly, bird meals mostly, a peck here and a peck there. Dirty blond hair, hadn't seen a shampoo in a month of Sundays. It carried the smells of the diner: eggs, bacon, coffee, the Virginia Slims Vera inhaled in the back alley whenever she got two minutes to herself. Vera wasn't pretty, and never had been. The wrinkles she'd acquired in the past few years were crueler than God's original mess-up of her face. But none of that mattered. She was efficient in her job, somewhat friendly, always turned on and aware. You had to have that—awareness—working the late shift, when all the crazies stumbled into the diner.

The place had taken two falls in the seven years Vera'd worked there. Guys had come in with pump-action shotguns the second time. Like something from a movie. Vera couldn't figure out how anyone could be so dumb and reckless, taking out a diner early in the a.m., when there were mostly singles and fives in the cash drawer, officers in and out for coffee. It took the police less than an hour to haul those two dummies in and book 'em. It hadn't taken much effort at all. Vera'd kept calm through the entire ordeal, came out of it unharmed. She'd shown up early for her next scheduled shift, as usual, already worn to the bone as she walked in the door.

Vera was thinking about all that when two more patrons walked in. The chimes above the door jingled. Vera looked up and surveyed the damage to come. Turned on and aware, as always, she figured these two wouldn't pose much problem. Big black guy who looked to be in his late thirties or early forties at most; you couldn't really tell with the blacks because they aged so gracefully. He could have been fifty for all Vera knew. What was that saying she'd heard? It was so spot-on she'd said she'd never forget it, and yet here she was reaching back to find it. Oh yeah, *Black don't crack*. It didn't, either. Vera envied that about them. White cracked like a lightbulb that fell and hit the floor. Roll of the dice what life you were granted, Vera supposed.

With the guy was a young girl, definitely in her teens, all full of innocence. Beautiful girl, Vera noticed, but something off about her, too. It was in the girl's eyes. Vera recognized that look. She'd spotted it in her mirror more times than she cared to admit.

Vera directed the two of them to a corner booth. She watched intently as they took their seats. The guy had this smile on his face that wouldn't quit. The girl couldn't return it. Couldn't. Not wouldn't. Couldn't. She didn't have the strength or desire to even try.

What's up with them? Vera wondered.

Daddy-and-daughter squabble? She wanted her friends over for a pajama party and then the Hannah Montana concert the next day, Daddy wanted her completing her trig homework and folding the laundry?

Could that be it, something like that?

Vera knew better.

It was all right there if you paid attention to the signs. Vera read 'em like tea leaves. How he kept his gaze on the girl—it was almost uncomfortable. And more telling, how the girl fought so hard not to look at him in return. There was tension there. Sadly, Vera noticed, it was of a sexual nature. Not good.

Vera decided right then she'd keep a close eye on them.

Wasn't twenty minutes later, Vera was at their table for about the fiftieth time. "Freshen up that coffee, sir?"

He nodded, slid his saucer to the table edge. Vera poured his coffee, her free hand on the small of her back. She had back troubles to go with her bad feet. Breaking down, falling apart, and didn't have much to show for all the trouble. Johnny, her oldest boy, was locked up. Shawn, the youngest, would be in a couple years, too. *These are the breaks,* Vera thought.

Vera asked the girl, "How are those eggs?"

The guy spoke for her. "She let 'em get cold."

"Something heavy on your mind, I see," Vera said to the girl. "You've been kind of just sitting here, staring."

The guy again: "Teens. You know how they are. You think I can get a slice of that apple pie?"

Vera wanted to hear from the girl. She asked her, "What about you, sweetheart? Want some dessert?"

The guy said, "She's fine."

Vera kept her gaze on the girl, waited. Finally the girl looked up at Vera and shook her head. Vera moved from the table, cussing under her breath, having a good mind to add a little something extra to that jerk's apple pie. Something not too nice, either. *Hey, Mom, what's for dinner? Go up your nose and pick a winner.* Something like that.

Vera was back in a snap with his pie. She hadn't done anything to it, which really bothered her, but that wouldn't have been right, she reasoned. *"Two wrongs never make a right,"* as her mother used to say. Vera cleared away the plate of eggs the girl hadn't eaten. "Can I get you folks anything else?" Everything she said was really directed at the sad girl.

The guy said, "Just the check."

Vera didn't want them to go.

She reached into her apron pocket anyway, took out the check slip and dropped it on the table. Offered a weak,

"Thanks for coming in. Hope you come back. I trust you enjoyed the food."

The guy said, "I did."

Nothing from the girl.

Vera moved away quickly. Passed an old black man at the counter putting a hurting on his food, some teen boys huddled in a corner booth freestyle rapping. Vera fumbled in her apron pocket for her pack of Virginia Slims. Two cigs left. She needed to kill the habit, save herself the money. How many new pairs of sneakers could she buy with the money she blew shredding her lungs?

Oh well.

She disappeared to the alley to calm her nerves with a smoke.

She set fire to it quickly, pretended she didn't smell the trash.

When she went back in, she headed directly to the booth where the guy and young girl had been. He'd placed the money and check under a saltshaker. Left an eighteen-dollar tip on a twelve-dollar order.

Hush money?

Vera felt dirty taking it.

The wannabe rappers called for her. She moved to them. "What you need?" But her mind wasn't really on them. She caught a glimpse of the guy who'd been with the young girl, standing outside on the curb, alone.

Vera said, "What happened to the girl?"

"She in the bathroom," one of the rappers said.

Vera hadn't realized she'd spoken aloud. All of this was really getting to her.

She said, "What?"

"That fine lil' bitty in the bathroom," the boy replied. "I'd try and talk to her when she comes out, but her pops don't look like he having it. And I ain't trying to fight off nobody's pops just to kick it with some ho."

I believe the children are our future, Vera thought.

She headed to the bathroom, ignored the disrespectful rapper's call of "Hey, lady, I wanted another Coke."

The girl was sequestered in a stall, sniffling. Vera rapped on the door softly with her knuckles. Her hands were going bad, too. Arthritis wrecking everything. Didn't matter at the moment, though. Vera had more important matters to attend to. She rapped her knuckles on the stall a second time. A little more forcefully that go-round.

The sniffling stopped; girl didn't answer, though.

Vera said, "May I talk with you, sweetheart?"

No answer.

"I'd like to help you. If you open up and let me talk to you, I think I can."

Vera waited. An eternity, it felt like. "I'm not leaving. I can wait you out. I don't think Mr. Personality out there will be happy about you keeping him waiting." Vera felt bad about mentioning him, but that was the way to play this.

Finally the door opened. The girl huffed and puffed. "What?"

She was trying to be hard, Vera noticed, but she wasn't

really. Fragile. A bird with broken wings. Vera was determined to mend them.

Vera said, "You've been hurt." It wasn't a question.

The girl diverted her gaze.

"I'd like to help you. But you have to talk to me."

The girl cut her eyes Vera's way. "You can't help me." Her voice was so soft it broke Vera's heart.

Vera's heart was more handle-with-care than the girl's fragile voice.

Vera said, "Your stepfather?"

The girl shook her head. "My momma's boyfriend."

Vera nodded. "Was my stepfather did it to me."

Something awakened in the girl's eyes. "You?"

Vera nodded. "From the time I was twelve until just after my seventeenth birthday. Felt dirty for a long time. Blamed myself. Thought everyone else would, too. Like I couldn't tell anyone. They wouldn't believe me. They'd blame me for letting it go on so long. Sound familiar?"

The girl nodded. It was as if Vera knew the voices in her head.

Vera said, "None of that's true, though. It isn't your fault. No one will blame you. You've been victimized. But you have to speak up. Now."

"Can't."

Vera took her hand, tears in both of their eyes. A connection was formed. "You have to. If you want to get your life back. If you want to have a chance at being the little girl that you are. You have to. Now."

The girl sighed.

Vera said, "Like I told y'all out there, my name's Vera. What's your name?"

The girl said, "In my dreams I'm Sister." She smiled. "It's just me and Brother. Sister and Brother against the world. He's like my guardian angel."

Vera said, "Brother doesn't know what you're going through. Brother can't help you stop it, either. Can he?"

Sister shook her head. Brother sure couldn't help her.

Vera said, "Let me try again. What's your name?"

Sister went ahead and told her.

kenya

It was right there on my locker at school for everyone to see.

Someone had fashioned together the word with stickers, a different one in a different color for each letter. If it wasn't such an ugly word, and didn't cut me so deeply, I would have thought the design of it was pretty. A pink *S*, a blue *N*, a purple *I*, and on it went. I stared at it for the longest time. All kinds of noise around me, yet I felt like I was in a vacuum.

I was alone.

No one was speaking to me.

All day I'd been ignored.

Sonya Riley rolled her eyes when I spoke to her first thing that morning, Misha Taylor smirked at my "Hey, girl!" and didn't open her mouth to speak back, and Essence Carter said something under her breath. I'm not sure what, but I know it wasn't nice.

Haters, I told myself.

But girls had always been a problem for me. Jealous 'cause I looked good, was smart, could sing, could move so nicely and make any song come to life, and all the boys loved them some Kenya. So even though their disses stung, I paid no attention to those fake girls. They could ignore me all they wanted. I didn't care.

But then Jamal Bryant walked by me like I was invisible, David Rivers let me know he couldn't care less what tidbits I had to share about Lark, and Dante Mosley told me matter-of-factly I wasn't "all that." I hadn't even asked Dante, or said anything to him; he just volunteered that hateful info.

I wasn't all that.

Seemed like everyone was making sure I knew it, too. Which brought about a crazy thought: was this how it was with Eric? I couldn't imagine having to endure this on a daily basis. I'd be ready to pull my hair out or hurt someone.

So I stomped to my locker with a purpose, set to retrieve my copy of *Beowulf* for English and determined to keep my head up, not let these haters see me sweat.

And there it was.

Oh hells no.

That hateful word spelled out with colorful stickers and plastered all over my locker for everyone to see. Somebody's idea of a joke, I guessed. It stopped me dead in my tracks. All my determination was gone. My legs turned to water. I couldn't keep my head up if I tried. And I didn't. I slumped my head and my shoulders. I was on the verge of tears.

"Snitch," came a voice from over my shoulder, reading the word on my locker.

Only one person in the school was still talking to me.

You could hear the hurt in his voice. My drama, and he'd taken ownership over it. What I went through, he went through. I was touched by that, but I couldn't let on.

Eric turned in a circle, yelled to everyone within earshot, "Whoever did this to my sister's locker is a savage. And a coward. Show your face, coward."

I didn't particularly like him putting me on blast as his sister.

I grabbed Eric's shoulder. "It's cool, Eric. Don't start something you can't finish."

"Letting these fools know—" and his voice amped up as he spoke to the hall crowd "—that you don't play that. And I don't, either. We're Poseys. Anybody got a problem with that…step up."

I pulled him close. "What's come over you, boy? You're causing a scene. Stop."

He whispered, "There are some things you don't know about me. I got peoples that have my back." He touched his neck when he said that. I noticed the edges of a chain but couldn't see it good because he had it tucked in his shirt. It was thick, I could tell, and looked like platinum. I couldn't believe it. Since when did my brother rock ice?

I wanted to ask him about it but didn't. Instead, I studied my runt of a brother and asked, "You've got peoples?"

He nodded.

I said, "I hope your peoples are providing you with health insurance."

"Aflac," he said, smiling.

He said it like the duck in the commercials. That was my brother, corny as all get-out. Still, I couldn't help laughing. He had no idea how much I needed to laugh at that moment. It really put me at ease. I'd forever love him for that moment. Even if I never shared with him how much it meant to me. Some things you had to keep close to the vest. Letting your little corny brother know how important he was to you being one of those things.

Eric moved beside me, leaned against a neighboring locker. "Good to see you laughing, Kenya."

I said, "To keep from crying."

He got a distant look in his eyes. "I heard that."

"Look, Eric." I didn't quite know where to begin. I reached deep down inside myself, came up with, "I'm sorry."

He could have milked it. Asked me what I was sorry for. He didn't. He simply nodded.

I asked, "How do you deal with this?"

"Dunno, Kenya. Just do."

"It's only been one day, and yet…it's been so hard for me."

He repositioned himself against my locker, seemed to consider something for a moment, and then said, "Regardless of how these kids treat me, I know I have value. I know I can be corny, but I'm worth something. That's what I force myself to remember while they're laughing at me, teasing me, beating me up. It can be hard to remember that sometimes, they can be so brutal, but…"

Our eyes were more than a little glassy.

Eric smiled, shook off any sadness, and looked at me. "Where's Lark?"

"Lark?" I'd forgotten about my closest friend. So self-absorbed I'd become.

Eric added, "Didn't see her yesterday or today."

I said, "I have to call her, see what's up."

We let thoughts of Lark settle between us, and then I asked, "What's being said about me?"

"Kenya, leave it alone."

"I can handle it."

Eric sighed and shook his head. "Everybody knows Ricky got that girl pregnant. And they know you told her mama. You're a snitch in everyone's eyes. You know how much everybody loves Ricky around here."

I nodded. I'd gotten caught up in the hype, too. "Speaking of Ricky…where's he at? I haven't seen him around, either."

Eric shrugged.

I said, "Did I do the right thing?"

"Everyone hates you, Kenya. Your popularity is in the toilet. You can see what you've lost. But Ricky was out of control. And what he did to that girl was terrible. Imagine how she must have felt, handling all that responsibility alone. You have to weigh it, Kenya. Did you do the right thing?"

Sadly, I wasn't sure.

* * *

Getting a ride home after school was never a problem. Usually.

But everybody suddenly had amnesia, and no ride was available to me.

Kenya who?

The popular girl.

One of the flyest chicks in the school.

Could sing like Keyshia Cole.

Dance like Ciara.

Her.

She didn't exist any longer. No one was impressed by me. No one cared about me.

I was stuck walking home.

And I wasn't happy about it. My walk was more of an angry march than anything else. I marched like that, lost in my own world. I'd just rounded the corner from our school when the toot of a horn startled me more than a little bit. I turned to see who was beeping at me, ready for some stuff. I'd been through more than I could handle. I was ready to spit in somebody's face if need be. I knew that wasn't a ladylike notion, but whatever. That was what it had come to.

When I saw who was idling in the car at the curb, I couldn't believe it. He had some nerve. I turned without speaking and restarted my angry march home.

His car rolled slowly next to me. "My bad, Kay," he said. "I didn't mean to startle you."

I kept walking but yelled to him, "Don't ever call me that again."

The car kept up its slow roll. I fought hard to outpace him. But I couldn't.

"Get in. This is too far of a walk for a diva like you."

I ignored him.

Damn right I was a diva.

"I'm not leaving your side, Kay. So you might as well get in."

I wheeled on him, angry. "I said, don't call me that."

Just then another car approached. Sebastian Wilson was at the wheel. His boy Franklin Gibbs was in the passenger seat. Carla Joy and Desiree Walker were in the backseat. They had room for one more. Sebastian had been trying to holla at me for the longest. I was just about to ask him for a ride when they all yelled out, "Snitch!" and peeled off. Their laughter and the sound of Sebastian's tires peeling rang in my ears. My eyes started to water, but I wouldn't let a tear fall. This other fool was still at the curb, watching me. I would not cry, especially not in front of him.

"Get in, Kay. You've had a tough time."

My voice was weak when I said, "Told you don't call me that."

He looked up the block, where Sebastian and his carload of haters had disappeared. "I could call you much worse. I think Kay's pretty nice."

I swallowed, moved to his car and got in. "Just take me home. Don't talk. I have nothing to say to you."

"Always the diva. But that's okay. You're a humbled diva, at least." He smiled. I wanted to wipe the smile off his face with the bottom of my shoe. Instead, I shot him an angry glare. He put his hand up in surrender and then pulled from the curb with the music on low.

I said, "Why you giving me a ride?"

"I thought we weren't going to talk. I'd gotten used to the idea." That smile again.

I said, "You make me sick, Donnell."

He laughed. "You fight it, but it's exactly the opposite. Your mind is forever in *hmm* mode, wondering about some Donnell."

I opened my mouth to cuss him out, but he put a finger to my lips. His finger was soft and warm. The profane words I had for him escaped me. My heart was doing something funny in my chest. My face flushed. He looked at me so deeply I felt naked. Yet I couldn't take my eyes off his. Donnell had always had some pretty eyes. You could get lost in them.

What was I doing?

Donnell noticed my reaction. His laugh was easy, confident. "See what I mean? I'm a biscuit, and you're desperately looking for some butter."

I said, "You make me sick, Donnell."

He laughed harder.

"You don't want to know what he had to say about you?" I shook my head to indicate I didn't. Donnell had already told me enough. Ricky had been forced to move down south, closer to Monique. His last year in school was totally disrupted. Monique's mom and Ricky's parents were bound and determined to hold him accountable. They weren't making him and Monique get married, but they let it be known they expected the two of them to raise their child together. Ricky's life had changed in a blink, thanks to my mouth. All the things he'd been accustomed to were gone. Parties at Donnell's. Too many girls to keep up with. Coming and going as he pleased. Even his car had to be sold to help with the bills a child brought. Ricky was set to be a teenage father. The load would be heavy.

I couldn't help feeling sad for him, even though he was the one who'd made that bed.

My inner Ne-Yo surfaced eventually, though. As much as I tried to fight it, I did wonder if Ricky thought of me anymore. And Donnell was my lifeline to my old love. I said, "Okay, I give. What did he have to say about me?"

Donnell said, "Said it to me, actually, but it involved you."

"Okay?"

"Ricky told me I was free to have you if I didn't care that you were his throwaway."

I was stunned.

That wasn't quite what I'd expected to hear.

Ricky saw me as a throwaway and nothing more.

Water found my eyes again.

I cried.

Donnell reached over and touched my shoulder. "I know that's painful to hear, Kenya. But that's how Ricky is. That's how little he really cared about you. I thought it was best if you knew the truth. Hoped it would help you move on. Not dwell on a relationship that was never good to begin with."

I shook my head. "He had some good points. He was tuned in to me, paid attention to the things I cared about. He cared about them, too, just because I did."

Donnell didn't say a word. He was probably wondering why I was still defending Ricky. I had to wonder myself.

I said, "He memorized a passage I loved in this old Toni Morrison book."

Donnell smiled, said, "'Milkman lay quietly in the sunlight, his mind a blank, his lungs craving smoke. Gradually his fear of and eagerness for death returned.' *Song of Solomon,* correct?"

I hunched my eyes in surprise. "How did you...?"

"You checked it out of the library. I saw you reading it, checked it out after you. You marked in the book, on that page, that passage. I know your handwriting." He smiled sheepishly, went on with, "I figured you must really like it. I memorized it."

"But Ricky..." I didn't know what else to say. I was dumbfounded.

"Ricky came to me wanting to get back in your heart. I told him some things I thought might help. That passage was one of them. It was some serious work to get him to remember those couple lines. Ricky's head is hard as brick."

Donnell laughed.

I didn't.

I said, "You helped him?"

Donnell gulped, nodded. "Hardest thing I ever did. But for some reason you really liked the dude. And I could see that you were hurting. So…"

So he helped Ricky to help me.

That was a huge sacrifice, considering how much he cared about me himself. There are so many definitions of love. So many ways we define it, describe it, explain it. I didn't truly have a grasp on it until that moment.

Donnell said, "I'm sorry I took part in deceiving you. Thought I was helping. I tried to warn you. Told you he was a player and that you'd get hurt. But, well, you had your own idea on things."

Through sobs, I said, "I'd punch him in the nose if I saw him."

Donnell laughed. "I did that already."

"What?"

He shrugged. "When he disrespected you like that, calling you a throwaway…I lost my cool. He's my boy and all, but I laid him out. Put him flat on his back."

I looked at Donnell with nothing but appreciation.

My sobs stopped. My eyes dried.

"Wanna come in for a bit?"

Donnell said, "Absolutely."

"Cool."

"But I won't."

I couldn't believe it. "What?"

"You're vulnerable."

I was.

He said, "I could take advantage."

"Maybe I want to be taken advantage of, Donnell."

He nodded. "Maybe you do, Kenya. But I'm not going to be the one to do it."

This boy was amazing.

I couldn't wait to tell Lark.

Donnell said, "Can I call you?"

"You have to ask?"

He smiled again. I could get used to his smile. It was so full of warmth.

He said, "Okay, I'll give you a call. Keep your head up."

I went to move and then turned back. I'd thought of something. I said, "Hey, Donnell?"

"Wassup, Kenya?"

"You can call me Kay."

I turned and rushed inside before he could reply.

I had a feeling he was smiling, though.

I took that name, that expression of regard for me, and I flipped it. I wasn't going to let it run negative through my mind. I was taking it back. I was Kay. Ricky just messed that up. But I *was* somebody's Kay, for sure. Like my brother had said earlier, I had value. I was somebody's Kay.

Donnell's, maybe. Time would certainly tell.

Mama was right; God works in mysterious ways.

Eric

I **don't** have shackles on my ankles, and my wrists aren't bound by the cool metal of handcuffs, but I feel like a prisoner on death row taking that final walk. I want to hope. I want to believe. But it's hard. Sometimes I feel as if hope is just something you read about in a novel or see in a movie. As if hope doesn't exist in the real world.

Mr. Quigley, the school's head hall aide, has been assigned the duty of escorting me safely from the building.

"These kids should be ashamed of themselves," he says.

For what they say to me or what they do to me? I wonder. Then I realize, *for both.* My white shirt is stained with mustard and ketchup. Several kids splattered me with open packets of the condiments during lunch. Another kid smacked the back of my head with a thick textbook from a class he's failing. Some girl poked my butt with a pin she pulled from a little Coach purse. Someone put stickers all over my locker like they'd done to Kenya's. Instead of being a snitch, they let me know I was *lame*.

The insults and teasing are worse today than ever. No one is sparing me today because I have a popular big sister. Kenya's popularity fell like the Dow Jones on Black Monday, and so I'm open to any humiliation the kids want to dole out. It's been attack day on the Poseys. On days like this I wish I was born a Clinton or a Kennedy. Shoot, even a Bush.

I look out at the street, the long walk of sidewalk before it reaches the curb. It's the same area where my face and Crash's fist made their acquaintance. There's a group of kids out there, loitering, in my opinion, as if they're waiting for me to come out. What they have in store for me I don't know. But after the day I've had, I imagine it isn't good.

Still, I tell Mr. Quigley, "I got it from here."

"Just gonna walk you out," he says.

"I'd rather you didn't. I'm fine."

"Eric."

"Just make things worse for me," I say, "if they see you walking me out like I'm in kindergarten."

He says, "I have a responsibility to see that you're safe."

I look out the door. A hundred paces. Not far at all. "I'll be fine."

"I'm gonna stand here and watch. If anything jumps off, I'm coming out."

I look at him. He's on the north side of fifty years old. Probably started graying at thirty, judging by the near-complete whiteness of his hair. Somewhat fit, I guess, but with a fullness to his belly that Crash probably won't get until he's in his seventies, if then. Even when Mr. Quigley frowns, he doesn't look mean. Everyone in the school listens to him, for the most part. But the kids don't listen because he's an imposing figure. We listen out of respect, because he reminds us of our grandfathers.

I can't have my grandfather rescue me and ever expect things to improve.

"I've got to handle this myself, Mr. Quigley."

His jaw sets but he nods. "If it gets hairy for you out there, I'm coming out, Eric. Tell you that now. I could give a crap about peer pressure and all that foolishness. How it makes you look. You're not getting hurt on my watch."

I say, "It's not that serious."

He eyes me, says nothing.

I turn back to the door, pause, and then step out. My heartbeat is strong in my ears, like the day Crash and I fought. My palms are sweaty but my mouth is dry. I take a deep breath and head down the sidewalk.

I can't be afraid. I can't live in fear.

The kids out front turn and watch me approach. I can see their mouths moving as they elbow one another and nod in my direction. I don't know what they're saying exactly, but I can guess.

I'm twenty paces away from them.

I can finally hear their words: *lame, Poser.*

That's the usual assortment of put-downs, so I'm not surprised.

I keep walking. I have to pass them to get to the curb.

They're lined up the same as the day Crash and I fought, like a *Soul Train* line, groups of them on both sides of the walkway with a clear path down the middle.

I move along that clear path.

One of the boys nudges me into a boy on the other side. He in turn nudges me into another boy. I'm a human pinball. Their laughter has the rhythm of music. I dance through them, get tossed from side to side as I pass.

I'm thankful Mr. Quigley doesn't come rushing out to defend my honor.

This isn't so bad.

At the curb is a black Range Rover, music rattling its tinted windows. Someone shoves me from behind, pushes me that much closer to the Range Rover. Mya comes strutting around the back of the truck. The boys behind me stop and stare. I know this without even looking back. The girls stop chewing their gum and do the same.

Mya's got her hair styled in two ponytails today. Pink boy shorts and a matching wife-beater show off her dazzling physique. She's got the type of body that makes something shift inside you. She smiles at me, comes up and pulls me into a deep embrace that is several notches above friendly. "What's good, baby boy?"

I don't really answer, say, "What's good with you?"

She squints, looks over my shoulder, then back at me as she says, "I'm good."

"You ready to roll, Mya?" I just want to get out of here.

She nods, says loud enough for the kids to hear, "Fiasco is waiting for you, baby boy."

I notice for the first time that she has a handful of CDs. She steps away from me with a presidential smile on her face, goes up to the kids who were tormenting me seconds ago.

She says to them, "You guys like Fiasco?"

Someone says, "The rapper?"

"Yup," Mya replies. "The one and only."

Several mingled voices, all of them excited, express that they love Fiasco.

Mya says, "Good. Here are some promotional CDs, guys. These are exclusives that aren't even on the radio yet. Y'all check 'em out. Hit up Fiasco's MySpace page if you're feeling it. Spread the word."

One of the boys says, "You know Fiasco?"

Mya nods, looks at me, and then back at the group. "Yeah, Fiasco's our homeboy."

Our.

Same boy asks, "Eric knows him, too?"

Mya smiles, doesn't answer, turns and makes her way back in my direction. "Come on, baby boy. Fiasco's waiting."

The boy calls out, "Hey, Eric. Holeup a sec, man. I need to talk to you about something."

I ignore him and move to Mya's Range Rover.

A girl calls out, "E. Where you headed?"

E.

Not *lame* or *Poser.*

That feels good. But I ignore her, as well, slide into Mya's whip.

Whip. I feel so cool right now.

Mya's back in the driver's seat. She gazes at me briefly, then puts the car in Drive and eases from the curb. I allow myself the victory of looking outside to see the expressions on the kids' faces. My classmates. Kids who have ignored me for years. Or if they weren't ignoring me, they were picking on me with reckless abandon. Everyone is standing at the curb watching me go. Wanting to be the kid shielded by tinted windows and sitting next to a woman as beautiful as a Pussycat Doll.

Wanting to be me.

It feels good.

I could get used to this.

"The ketchup and mustard?" Mya asks. "They did that?"

"They did that."

Mya falls into silence, her gaze on the road ahead of us, music off. She turned it off almost as soon as we got in and drove away from the school. She thrums her fingers on the steering wheel, bites her lip. Anxiety is all over her face.

I say, "It's okay. I'm fine."

She shakes her head and stays with her silence.

I say, "They're treating my sister bad now. That's not okay. I'm bothered by that. Kenya isn't use to it. I don't know how she's gonna handle it if it continues."

I tell her all about Kenya. My sister's rise and fall.

Mya smiles. "Keyshia Cole, huh?"

"Probably sings better. Kenya has an incredible voice. I could picture her doing background vocals on one of Fiasco's songs."

Mya frowns at that.

I say, "You have siblings?"

"A half brother."

"Where's he at?"

Mya says, "Fiasco says there's something special and pure about your heart. He's right. You go through all that—" she nods back in the direction of school "—and yet you're more worried about your sister than yourself. Talking to me about my life like you weren't assaulted today. That's what happened, you know? They assaulted you."

"It's cool."

"See what I mean?"

I say, "I try not to dwell on it. Don't make me out to be someone special."

"You are special, baby boy."

I nod. "Right now, yes. But only because I know Fiasco."

Mya frowns again. "Fiasco's human, just like you. Don't get fooled by all the hype."

"He's a good dude."

She nods. "For the most part. Wish he chose better company."

I say, "His crew, every last one of them is a thug."

Mya says, "Every last one of them…"

"Scary dudes."

"He grew up with them. He's loyal. To a fault."

"You don't like them, huh?"

"Some less than others."

"I know what you mean. I wouldn't catch myself dead around guys like them if it weren't for Fiasco."

She eyes me. "Don't idolize Fiasco, baby boy. That's a problem. He's a good guy, yes. For the most part, like I said. But you aren't special because you know him."

I say, "Okay. I'm special because I know you, then."

"Me?"

"Yeah, you. Don't act like you don't know you're…" I let the thought go. I'm trained to keep my praise of beautiful girls to a minimum. Usually, right after I've complimented them, they laugh at me or say something that crushes my spirit.

Not that I think Mya would do that.

Mya says, "I got teased all the time when I was in school. My parents made it a habit to drop me off at school and pick me up themselves. Every day. They felt it fostered family, kept us close, and plus they worried about me a lot. Kids called my pops Agent Orange and my mother a gook. They called me even worse. My pops was a veteran. Risked everything, put it all on the line for this country. And they disrespected him. I hated that. I was like you, baby boy. Tease me all they wanted, but leave my family alone."

I say, "You're black and Korean?"

Mya nods. "Guilty."

She adds, "Grew up down in Camden, for the most part. And down there, my fifty percent black was fifty percent too little. I got my ass beat for no reason at least once a week. I remember I got these door-knocker earrings 'cause all the girls were wearing them. They beat me up and took 'em. I had to lie to my parents that I lost them. I think they knew better."

"Man."

Mya says, "Then my father died and everything fell apart. Momma couldn't handle him gone. She couldn't handle my brother and me. She became a different person. Took up with the wrong kind of people." She pauses for just a sec and then continues with, "Between home and school I thought God must hate me for sure."

"Crazy."

Mya smiles, regroups. "Funny you should say that. I stood by and let the kids at school treat me any way they wanted for the longest. Then one day I couldn't take it anymore. Totally spazzed out. I picked up a chair and was just swinging that bad boy around, trying to connect with any- and everyone. I plowed down like five kids. After that, I was the crazy girl that no one messed with. I liked that. Stayed to myself. Which was fine."

I say, "Beautiful as you are, it's hard to picture you not fitting in."

Mya says, "You say the sweetest things, baby boy. Don't change. You're gonna make some girl really happy one day."

I look down at my lap. "Doubt it."

"Why you say that? You're a cute boy, you're gonna be handsome when you get bigger."

"Cute." I snort at the notion.

Mya looks over at me. "I said it. Cute. Ears a little too big for your head, but you'll grow into them."

"You're really helping. Thanks."

She laughs. "Just kidding you, baby boy. You're cute, I promise you."

I look out the window. I can't look Mya in the eye as I open myself up. It's so much easier to do without eye contact. "Sometimes I just want to cry when they pick on me. Just stop and let the tears flow. Let them know how much their teasing and picking hurts."

"That'd be the wrong move. They want to see you affected that much. They'd tease you worse if you did that."

"I know," I say. "That's why I don't do it. But the urge is strong, believe me."

Mya's quiet for a bit. Thinking, I suppose. Finally she says, "Look at me a sec."

I do.

"Okay, baby boy. Squint your eyes like you're having trouble seeing me."

I do.

"Not so much. As if your vision isn't twenty-twenty but you don't need a Coke bottle over your eyes, either."

I lessen my squint.

"That's it, Eric. Now…" She pauses, then, "Lean a bit

to the side with your arms crossed over your chest. And cock your head a bit to the side, too."

"What is all this?"

"Just do it."

I do.

She smiles wide. "You've got it, baby boy."

I ask, "Got what?"

"Your pose," she says, "for Fiasco's video."

Crawford's Corner Road is the cornerstone of a neighborhood that's perfect for raising a family. You can hear birds chirping in the morning, I bet. The roar of lawn mower engines, the whir of sprinklers. All the residences have mailboxes, and they're never vandalized, never broken into, and mail, especially checks, is never stolen from them. The people who live in the neighborhood have antique brooches, personal landscapers, large maples in their backyards, things of that sort.

Mya says, "Nothing like where I grew up."

"Me either."

She pulls into a property that's large even for this neighborhood. A mansion, far as I can tell. She parks and cuts the engine, the Range Rover one of about twenty vehicles clogging a circular cobblestone drive that butts the house.

"Fiasco lives here?"

"Rents it," Mya says. "March to August."

She steps out of the Range Rover. I follow. Instead of

walking in through the front door, she follows a path on the side of the house to the back. As we get close to the rear of the house, the chatter of voices and the swelling sounds of hip-hop music invade my ears.

Fiasco's Dirty Jersey crew is everywhere. They're on the grass, on the patio by the house, splashing in the pool. There's a gorgeous girl every few feet. A bikini is the attire of choice for most of them. I say *girl* because not one looks older than twenty or twenty-one.

Mya walks past several of Fiasco's boys, doesn't even acknowledge them as they call out her name.

She makes a beeline for Fiasco.

I see him, close to the pool, surrounded by a bevy of bikini'd beauties.

He's got a huge smile on his face.

I can't say I blame him.

But the smile fades as he spots Mya hard-strutting in his direction.

Mya barks, "Who's checking IDs?" as soon as she reaches him.

Fiasco says, "Checking IDs for what?"

"Play stupid and get the whole thing shut down. Lose everything you've worked so hard to build."

Fiasco frowns, starts to reply to Mya, but then spots me. "E.P.," he says, "you made it. You ready to be a star?"

The bikini girls eye me, wondering who I am to get such attention, I suppose. Mya does, too. She looks hurt that Fiasco tossed aside her concerns like dirty laundry. I want to shrink away. Disappear so Fiasco can resume the conversation with Mya.

Fiasco announces, "Everybody's here. Let's shoot ourselves a rap video."

Everyone cheers.

Everyone except Mya. And me.

It's closer to a movie than a rap video, though.

There's actual dialogue, actors and actresses, a plot, the whole nine.

And it's an exclusive situation. Very few people will ever get the opportunity to watch a video made, to see the process behind what ends up on MTV and BET. I stand in the shadows of the production. Behind me are the two big dudes from Fiasco's warehouse, Mr. Jets and the Black Fonz. Seeing the Black Fonz again makes me nervous. I can't help remembering him ushering those two young girls into the PRIVATE room. I can't help feeling threatened in his presence. But I fight the feeling.

Focus on the video being shot.

Fiasco is the lead, of course. Mya's his leading lady. They're shooting what is supposed to be an intimate bedroom scene. Incense sticks are lit, a pleasant vanilla musk scent. Candles are burning to enhance the dim lighting.

Everything is perfect.

Or almost everything is perfect.

The usual chemistry between Fiasco and Mya in his videos is missing. Mya would rather be anywhere in the world besides this video set. You can gather that from her expression and from her lack of warmth in what is supposed to be a romantic scene.

Fiasco feeds her fruit. Carefully fingers wedges of melon and cubes of pineapple between her luscious lips. She eats with her eyes closed.

Mya open her eyes and says, "Is that cayenne pepper?"

Fiasco says, "Yes," then stops dead in his tracks. A deep frown creases his forehead. He cocks his head to the side, does this angry thing with his lips I can't describe. "Wait a minute. Did you say 'cayenne pepper,' Mya? You're flubbing your lines now, too. I fed you *fruit* and you come up with 'cayenne pepper.' What is wrong with you, girl?"

The scene has completely broken down.

The director, a twentysomething black guy with a thick British accent, real name is Bartholomew something-or-other but everyone calls him The X-Treme, throws his hands up in frustration. He's too dramatic for my taste. He's more of a diva than my sister.

Fiasco says, "Mya."

She snaps, "What?"

"Time is money, girl."

"Ask me if I care."

There's a digital clock on the bedside table that reads 11:59 p.m. It's actually a quarter past four in the afternoon. Mama will be upset if I'm not home by six or seven o'clock. I'm known to spend time after school at the library, at Benny's, wherever, so Mama doesn't worry about me. I don't look for trouble and it doesn't generally find me, either. But I'm always home before dark. If I'm not today, and that looks possible, I will have a lot of explaining to do. Mama's been extra sensitive lately. Extra controlling. Extra demanding. Ever since our powwow in the kitchen, Mama's been on high alert. In her words, she will not "lose one or both" of her children. With things the way they are, I can't imagine what will await me if I walk through the front door of my house after the sun has set for the day. Still, I can't leave. This video is my opportunity. This is my big chance.

Fiasco reaches out to Mya, takes her hands. "I need you to work with me. You know how important this project is to me."

She shoots back, "You know how important certain things are to me, too, but did that affect your choices? I'll answer for you. It didn't."

Fiasco looks over at me. I straighten my posture. Is he looking to me to rectify this situation? Have I garnered that much weight in his life?

Fiasco calls out, "Alonzo, can you keep watch on the young heads outside, make sure they stay out of trouble, since we didn't check IDs?"

The Black Fonz, aka Alonzo, drifts away like a heavy wind.

Fiasco sighs, turns his attention back to Mya. "This project is important to me, Mya. I need it to go well. Please?"

Mya smiles; Fiasco mirrors her.

Then she says again, "Ask me if I care."

Fiasco's smile fades. Mya's holds.

The X-Treme throws his head back and cries out like someone struck him with something; he has a look on his face like he ate some bad seafood. The video shoot is falling apart. Just my luck. I get invited to be in a hip-hop video, a once-in-a-lifetime experience, and the whole thing is sinking like the *Titanic*. Just my luck.

Fiasco grinds his jaw, points an accusing finger at Mya. He says, "Girl...I swear."

Mya says, "You want to hit me? Do it. I can handle it. I can handle anything."

Fiasco balls his hand in a fist, pulls back his arm to throw a punch.

I hold my breath.

He's gonna hit Mya.

More Murdaa than Fiasco, that's what he is at the moment.

He holds the punch, though. Backs away. He moves over to a corner, pulls out his cell phone, presses it to his ear, and immediately starts in on an animated conversation with someone. Curses flow from his mouth.

The X-Treme goes over to Mya, starts talking to her. It's obvious he's pleading with her. Just as obvious, she's being difficult.

It's getting closer and closer to five. Mama will be livid if I don't walk in the door soon. I don't have many options. I came with Mya. I have no ride home.

I move toward her.

The X-Treme begs her not to "mash my video," in that annoying British accent. Pretense, I bet. He's probably from Trenton or something.

I say, "Mya?"

"Not now, Eric."

I'm not "baby boy" when she's angry, I guess.

"I need—"

She wheels on me. "What? You need what? What? What? What?"

I say, "Your cell phone. I have to make a call."

She marches over to a chair and snatches up her pocketbook and fumbles it open and pulls out her cell phone and tosses the pocketbook down and marches back over to me and angrily flips the phone at me.

It bounces off my fingertips and hits the floor.

Mya says, "Dayum," and turns her back on me.

The X-Treme resumes his begging.

I struggle to remember numbers I rarely dial, and then the memory part of my brain fires.

I get an answer on the third ring. "Yeah," the voice says. "Who is this?"

I say, "Kenya."

"Yeah?"

"It's me."

"Eric?"

"Yeah."

"Whose phone you calling from?"

I say, "Long story. I need a favor from you."

"Hmm. What?"

"Can you get one of your friends to give me a ride? I need to get home before Mama flips out."

Kenya says, "I don't have any friends to give you a ride."

I sigh.

She says, "Where you at?"

"You wouldn't believe me."

"Oh boy," Kenya says. "What mess you in, Eric?"

"I'm supposed to be in a video."

"What are you talking about?"

"You know Fiasco?"

"The rapper?"

I say, "Yeah."

"What about him?"

"I know him, Kenya. I met him a while back. I'm out at his place, supposed to be in his new video, but there's a problem."

Silence greets me on the line.

I say, "Kenya, you there?"

She says, "So it's true? I got a text from a former friend asking me about your being cool with Fiasco. I thought it was a joke."

News travels fast.

I say, "It's true."

"Why didn't you tell me?"

I don't have time for explanations. "Can you help me?"

"That's all you have to say on the matter?"

I say, "Yes."

Kenya huffs, "Where are you at?"

I tell her all the details about the property on Crawford's Corner Road.

She says, "I'll get Donnell to bring me."

"Oh, okay." *Wait a minute, hold up.* "Donnell Tucker? The boy you can't stand?"

"Yeah. And?"

"Nothing. Do you."

Dial tone greets me.

Donnell Tucker and Kenya in the same car.

And I'm walking away from the chance of a lifetime, the opportunity to be in a video that will probably be played all over MTV and BET.

Is the world upside down or what?

"You know this beautiful young lady?"

That's the Black Fonz. I nod in reply to his question, unable to open my mouth and speak. His presence is a dark cloud. When I look at him, all I see are those young girls being led into the PRIVATE room.

"Guess you're good, then, young lady," he says. "But I do have to pat you down. Security purposes, of course."

Kenya smiles at him like she's on a game show. She doesn't know what I know. The Black Fonz starts at her ankles, works his way up, lingers too long for my taste at her hips. He grazes over her upper body pretty quickly and then straightens. "You're good."

Kenya says, "Thank you."

"No. Thank *you*."

Again, Kenya smiles.

The Black Fonz leaves us be. We're just around the corner of the house, on the edge of the backyard. There are a few hangers-on still outside, but most everyone is in the house for the video shoot. I left, came outside after the drama between Fiasco and Mya unfolded. I care for them both. I hated to witness their meltdown.

Kenya grips my arm. "This place is off the chains."

I nod. "It's very nice."

Her grip tightens on my arm. "Where's Fiasco?"

"Inside, I believe."

"Take me."

I say, "We need to get home."

Kenya bats her eyes, gives me a hug and rests her head on my shoulder. "Please." She must think I'm Donnell Tucker.

I want to go. I don't want to disappoint or upset Mama. I say, "Donnell brought you?"

Kenya removes her head from my shoulder. A big smile graces her face. I've never seen her happier. "Yeah. Ain't that crazy?"

"What happened with you two?"

Kenya shrugs. "I stopped running."

"Where's he at?"

She frowns, says, "Out front waiting in his car."

I say, "He—"

Kenya cuts me off with, "Stop playing, Eric. I want to meet Fiasco. Please."

She says it with such passion, such desperation. For once I'm what she needs. I say, "Follow me."

I lead her inside. Take her to the bedroom. Fiasco isn't there. Mya, either. The X-Treme is sitting in his director's chair, swilling a Mug root beer like it's a Heineken. I ask him, "Where's Denzel?"

He looks up at me. His eyes are red. I suspect he's been crying. He looks at Kenya, then me again. Confusion is all over his face. He asks, "Who? Denzel?"

I say, "Fiasco, the leading man."

The X-Treme sniffs. Motions toward the other side of the house. He's back drowning his sorrows in the twenty-ounce bottle of Mug before I can ask another question. I leave him be, head in the direction he pointed me. Kenya's on my heels like a puppy.

Glass doors lead to an outside patio I hadn't noticed before. I see Fiasco out there by himself. I slide the door open, usher Kenya through first, and then step out myself. I close the door behind me. Fiasco has his back to us. He doesn't turn around to see who's invading his space.

I say, "Fiasco?"

He grunts in answer but still doesn't turn around.

"Like you to meet my sister."

At that he finally turns, slowly. His eyes are red like The X-Treme's. To my surprise, a white plume of smoke circles Fiasco's head. My first thought is he's been smoking weed, but then I notice the brown-on-white two-tone of his cigarette, the green and white box of Newports clutched in his hand.

I say, "Didn't know you smoked."

He says, "I didn't know it, either," then drops his cigarette and stomps it out. A ready smile comes to his face. He moves to Kenya, a hand outstretched. "I didn't know E.P. had such a pretty sister. You a straight banger, ma."

If Kenya was Christina Aguilera, her cheeks would be fire-engine red. She says, "Yeah, I'm a... I'm... I'm E.P.'s older sister."

"Y'all close?"

Kenya says, "Tighter than Wayne and Birdman."

Fiasco chuckles. "Aiight, now. You like hip-hop, too?"

Kenya says, "Fo' sho'."

My mouth drops open. Kenya hates rap.

Fiasco says, "Your brother here is a rap aficionado. Even knows stuff from before his time."

Kenya nods. "He's a Wikipedia entry when it comes to rappers. Ask him anything about hip-hop and he's got an answer. I love that."

I say, "Now, Kenya."

She ice grills me. I keep my mouth shut. She cooks pancakes on Saturday mornings, per our Mama, and I don't want anything other than the occasional chocolate chip added to the buttermilk batter.

Fiasco says, "I had a scene in the video for Eric, but I hear he's leaving."

Kenya says, "Yeah."

Fiasco frowns. "That's too bad. I could have worked you in as an extra, Kenya."

Kenya looks at me. "I'll handle Mama. We're staying."

My twin has spoken.

Fiasco says, "This video gonna revolutionize the game."

It's been a good shoot thus far, even with the absence of Mya. Fiasco used a different girl, obviously not as pretty as the Black-Korean bombshell, as a fill-in. And Kenya got to strut her stuff in the background for a ten-second pool scene.

I say, "It's tight. It's something the young heads need to see. Love enduring. Everybody's afraid to love nowadays, all you see is ice grills and hate. That's it." I talk so much cooler when I'm around Fiasco. And it comes out so naturally. It's amazing how much positive influence he has over me.

Fiasco nods at my little speech, yells to The X-Treme, "Aiight, let's get the B-side flowing. Bring in the gangstas, Mr. Director." Fiasco's excitement is palpable. He half sings, "It's Murdaa."

The X-Treme directs somebody else to bring in the gangstas.

Fiasco says, "You ready, E.P.?"

"What's going on?"

Fiasco says, "I came up with the idea to do a promotional video with both my projects on it. A combo platter with both Fiasco and Murdaa."

I say, "What?"

Fiasco nods. "And you, son, are gonna represent for the Murdaa part. I'm gonna get your street cred up, too."

I say, "What? What I'm gonna do?"

Fiasco smiles, says, "You're gonna be a gangsta, son."

I'm too surprised to speak.

"I can't be a gangsta, Fiasco. I don't know how."

He touches my shoulder. "You can and you will."

A young lady comes over as if on cue, hands me a bandanna and a tire iron. There's another girl with her. The other girl hands her a pair of baggy jeans and a white tee. She then hands me those items as well. It takes two to get anything done on set. I've learned that today during my brief introduction to Hollywood.

I look at the items in my hands for some time. What do I do with them?

Fiasco says, "Get changed, E.P."

I manage, "What?"

Fiasco says, "Tie the bandanna around your head. Juelz Santana style."

"Gonna need help with that."

"You've got to be joking."

I say, "I'm a little rusty tying bandannas."

Fiasco directs the girl who handed me the items to come back over. He tells her, "Thug my boy out."

She takes me to a dressing area. At her direction I step behind a partition and slide on the jeans, ease into the white tee. Dressed, I come back out with the bandanna still in my hand. She ties it on my head, adjusts it, then stands back to look me over. She says, "Untuck your chain, and let it hang low to your chest."

I do as she says.

"You so thugged out it's ridiculous," she says approvingly.

Thugged out?

Me?

Hard to imagine.

She walks me over to a full-length mirror they have set up. I blink several times. My eyes have to be playing tricks on me. I look cooler than I've ever looked before. The jeans fit just right, with a perfect sag. The white tee is snug, and my arms are skinny, for sure, but more muscular than I ever noticed. I've got a chiseled skinny-boy body that isn't half-bad. And the bandanna is a perfect touch.

Bye, Steve Urkel.

I say, "I look…"

"Cool," she finishes.

The X-Treme says, "Roll tape."

Fiasco stands directly across from me.

A scowl paints his face.

He's dressed in black cargo pants that fall way below his hips, a fresh pair of Timbs and a white wife-beater that shows off his lean physique. I'm in the baggy jeans from wardrobe, an interesting pair of gray Timbs and a white tee. They had me jettison the tire iron—overkill according to The X-Treme.

Fiasco stands with his feet shoulder-width apart, arms crossed in front of him. I squint like I'm having trouble seeing. Not too much, though. Not like I need Coke bottles over my eyes. I lean a bit to the side with my arms crossed over my chest. And cock my head a bit to the side, too. It's a cool pose. It's Mya's. She deserves all the credit.

Fiasco eyes me with poise and calm. That's a feat, because I'm flanked by ten sho' nuff thugs. We have him boxed into a corner. He doesn't seem fazed in the least.

If this were a real-life scenario and I was in Fiasco's position, I'd be dripping with sweat. My heart would be in my throat. My stomach would be in knots. Fiasco is cool as can be, though. He's tough and defiant despite the long odds against him.

He says, "My heart don't pump fear," and reaches for his waist.

The X-Treme yells, "And...cut. That's a wrap, brethren."

An abrupt end, but they piece things together and make a whole later, so I'm not surprised.

The video is done. I can't wait to see it.

Fiasco comes over to me, touches my shoulder, says, "I'm having them leak this to YouTube in the next few hours. You're about to be a star, E.P. A star, ya heard?"

Bye, Steve Urkel.

Hello, fifteen minutes of fame.

kenya

"YouTube. YouTube. YouTube. Anyone in this school care about anything else?"

"I guess I know who drank all the Hatorade."

"Whatever, Donnell. You make me sick."

Of course he smiled at that. Swore he was cute, which he was, but whatever. I needed his moral support. I needed to be comforted. Life kept on handing me lemons and I didn't have the strength to make lemonade.

Lark said, "You should be happy for Eric, Ken. I know I am."

"I liked you better when you weren't here, Lark."

She said, "Nice, Ken. Real nice."

I knew it wasn't. She'd just gotten back to school after a bout with chicken pox. Or was it poison ivy? Bird flu? Whatever, it was something. And it'd kept my girl away from me for over a week. I'd only made it through that time because so much drama was happening in my life. I didn't need to treat her badly as much as I needed her.

I told her, "Sorry. I'm just bummed. Life is treating me like I'm Britney Spears right about now."

"Don't be so dramatic, Ken."

Donnell said, "Yeah."

I looked at him hard. Let him know I wasn't in the mood. He smiled at me. But I wouldn't soften.

I said, "I'm in the video, looking cute as all get-out."

Donnell said, "I'm sure. And I was sitting in the car twiddling my toes."

I didn't pay that any mind. You want me, you gotta work.

Lark said, "I know that's right, girl."

I poked out my lips, said, "Then why didn't Fiasco leak the whole video?"

Lark said, "It'll be out there soon, I'm sure."

Donnell added, "Yeah. The YouTube thing's just a teaser to whet folks' appetites."

I looked around. Kids were moving by swiftly without speaking a word to me. I wasn't used to that. I could never get used to that. I needed that video with me in it out there pronto.

Lark said, "People are buzzing about the YouTube, Ken. When the whole thing comes out, you are gonna blow up."

I doubted it.

My little ten seconds wasn't much. But it was enough, I guessed, to get me back in the good graces of my school-mates. That would be enough for me.

Meanwhile, Eric, my pain-in-the-behind of a brother, was on full blast all over YouTube. The two-and-a-half-minute clip that Fiasco leaked boasted more than a minute of Eric playing gangsta. I didn't think much of his acting skills personally, but whatever.

Lark said, "Eric's eating this all up. He was so cute earlier. He had a crowd of girls around his locker and he did this word-of-the-day bit. It was crazy."

I'd heard about it. I didn't care to listen to the story again. So I opened my locker and made busy reorganizing my textbooks.

Donnell said, "Word of the day? What was that about?"

I tried to drown them both out but couldn't.

Lark's tone rose. "Oh, it was too funny, D. His word was *inward*."

"Inward?"

Lark nodded, laughed, composed herself and then went on. "Yeah. *Inward*. And then he used it in a sentence."

Donnell said, "What he say?"

I couldn't help looking closely at Donnell. His eyes were wide with anticipation. At the moment I couldn't believe I'd fallen for him.

Lark cracked up again, got caught in a coughing spell. And she accused me of being dramatic? Please. I wasn't about to pat her back, that was for sure.

Donnell did, though. They both laughed together.

Calm, Lark said, "Eric's crazy, D, I'm telling you. He was so serious. I saw a side of him today I never knew existed. He was so confident, so assured. He said 'inward.' And then he paused, like a showman. His sentence was, 'I'ma black out on anyone that calls me the inward.'"

Donnell got himself a coughing spell.

Lark said, "Get it? *Inward.* N word."

Donnell just nodded, couldn't even speak.

What in the world was I doing with that boy?

Donnell managed, "He said 'black out'?"

Lark couldn't even answer. She just nodded.

I left them there acting like my brother was just the cleverest thing.

They didn't even realize I'd stepped away.

Lil' Wayne and Birdman's "Pop Bottles" cried out from my hip. I was surprised to hear that ringtone. Surprised and nervous. I fumbled for my cell phone, flipped it open on the fourth ring. Just in time, as it flows into voice mail on the fifth.

I said, "Holla."

"What's up?"

"Oh, hey. Wassup?" I tried to stay calm. Played that role lovely.

"Nada. Got some free time. You want to hang out?"

Did I wanna be next to Fiasco?

Hmm, let me see.

Hells yeah, I did.

I said, "I can swing that."

"You at school now?"

"Yup."

"What time you get out?"

I said, "Three-fifteen."

"Twenty minutes."

I said, "You can come scoop me up?"

"On it like white on rice. I'll be out front of your school when you get out."

I said, "What you pushing?"

He said, "Black Land Rover."

Eric

"Hey, E, I'm having a party this weekend. Wanna come?"

"Hey, E, Tammy Morgan told me to give you her number."

"Eric, where you get them Wallabees? They're mean, son."

"Hey, E, we 'bout to hit the mall. You wanna rock with us?"

"E, I sent you a MySpace message this morning. You get it?"

"E, approve me as your MySpace friend, please. Put me in your top ten. Okay? Okay, E?"

It was too much.

Making it out of the school building isn't easy. Every step I take, someone stops me, asks me a question, asks me for a favor, begs me for something, invites me somewhere.

I step around a crowd of boys and girls, make my way

to the front door. I'm exhausted. I want to get home and take a nap.

You believe that? A nap in the middle of the afternoon. That's how it is, though. Being popular is work. I got worked over like a one-legged slave today.

Smiling.

Telling jokes.

Posing for cell phone pictures.

Listening.

I think I might have even kissed a few babies.

I have my hand on the door now, an inch away from opening it. When I get outside, I'm going to run without stopping until I reach home.

I'm one inch to daylight, to freedom.

I hear, "Eric?"

No. No. No.

I start to take off running anyway. Pretend I didn't hear my name called.

"Eric?"

Shoot.

I turn around.

Mr. Quigley's smile is crooked but pleasant.

I say, "Yes, Mr. Quigley?"

He says, "Just wanted to see if I could touch the hem of your garment."

He laughs.

I wave him off.

He says, "No, in all seriousness, I'm glad the tide has turned."

"Thanks."

"Be good."

I take that good wish and step outside, finally. Coast is clear for the most part. A few kids are scattered about, but they're so busy in conversation they don't notice me. I better go quick before they catch a glimpse of me; then it'll be elbows touching sides, heads nodding in my direction, the vultures descending on me.

I look up and see Kenya running toward the street. A black Land Rover idles at the curb. Fiasco? What's he doing here? I stop and watch Kenya's determined trot. Her cell phone slips from her purse, clacks against the pavement.

I yell out, "Hey, Kenya?"

She turns, sees me, waves, and then keeps going. I run to try and catch up. "Kenya, wait. You dropped your phone."

Either she doesn't hear me or she doesn't care. She slides into Fiasco's Land Rover. I reach down and pick up her phone. Just like her to be selfish, to try to elbow her way in on my friendship with Fiasco. I should toss her cell phone in the woods somewhere. As much as she loves this thing, that would hurt, teach her a lesson about staying in her place. How dare she step to Fiasco behind my back?

The Land Rover pulls off.

I watch it go.

kenya

"**Your** brother's gonna be mad we took off like that."

I said, "He'll get over it."

"How was school?"

I thought about all the love Eric got, the apathy that came my way. I said, "Sucked."

"Really?" He widens his eyes in surprise. "Why's that?"

"Just going through some things."

He tapped his large hands on the steering column. "I imagine the boys must drive you crazy."

"How so?"

He looked over at me. I swear his eyes drifted over my whole body, seemed to linger on my chest. I shifted in my seat. He sniffed out a laugh, kept his gaze on me. "You're a ripe piece of fruit, girl. Boys wanna get their fingers slick with that juice, right?"

I didn't like that comment one bit. I wasn't going there with him.

I said, "We're going back to the mansion?"

He shook his head.

I said, "Where?"

"Chillax, Kenya."

I frowned. "What?"

He smiled. I saw the devil in his countenance. He said, "I heard a young person say that once. Chillax. *Chill* and *relax* combined, you get it?"

I got it.

I reached in my purse, felt around. Oh hells no. Why was this happening?

I asked, "Can we turn around? I left my cell phone somewhere."

He looked over at me, smiled again. His teeth looked too perfect. Dentures, falsies, I guessed. He said, "Don't even sweat that phone, Kenya."

The way he said my name made my skin crawl.

I started to feel tight around the neck. My heartbeat was a runaway locomotive. I said, "We meeting up with Fiasco?"

He took that moment to turn on the stereo. It wasn't my kind of music, but I knew who it was. Marvin Gaye.

I repeated, "We meeting up with Fiasco?"

He turned the volume up, didn't answer me.

I said, "Mr. Alonzo?"

He still didn't answer, didn't even look in my direction.

"Mr. Alonzo... Mr. Alonzo... Mr. Alonzo... Mr. Alonzo..."

Eric

AS tired as I am, sleep just won't come. My room is dark, quiet, and yet sleep just won't come. I jump out of bed, giving up on sleep, and turn on the television. Straight to BET—*106 & Park* is on. Rocsi and her fine self. She's doing a little dance with the day's guest: Wyclef.

Kenya's cell phone rings for the millionth time. Someone's really been blowing her up. She's not even popular at the moment and her phone still rings off the hook. I've never even thought about having one myself. Who would call? Benny?

But maybe I should reconsider. I'm on the verge of having some long-term popularity. If Kenya doesn't mess things up for me.

I can't believe she hooked up with Fiasco without me. She wouldn't even know him if I hadn't made the introduction. I can't believe he would meet with her behind my back, that he'd drive off without any consideration for me.

I walk over and pick up Kenya's phone from my dresser, scroll through her "received" calls until I find the number I want. I dial it without hesitation.

She picks up right away.

I say, "Mya?"

"Baby boy?"

"Oh, I'm baby boy again?"

"I acted a fool, I'm sorry. I got caught up with some emotions. You wouldn't understand."

I say, "Yeah, you did."

I hear the smile in her voice. "I heard you killed."

I say, "Did you see it?"

"Not yet. Couldn't even look at it. It's on YouTube, right?"

"Yeah."

She says, "I'll check it out eventually."

I ask, "You and Fiasco make up?"

"Haven't talked to him. No."

Should I tell her?

I don't want to hurt her.

But I'd want to be told if the shoe were on the other foot.

I say, "Your boyfriend picked my sister up from school today."

Mya doesn't say anything.

I say, "You heard me?"

"I did."

"You and Fiasco have a weird relationship."

"My half brother."

I say, "What?"

"Fiasco is my brother."

I'm stunned.

I don't know what to say.

Mya talks for me. "He's stupid. How old is your sister?"

I manage, "Seventeen."

Mya tsks. "And he came to school and picked her up?"

"Yup. Pulled up in a black Land Rover."

Mya says, "Range."

I correct her. "Nah, it was a Land."

Her tone changes. "You're sure?"

"Yeah. I saw it at the warehouse. It's a Land."

"Oh my God!"

I ask, "What's wrong? You okay, Mya?"

She says, "That's not Fiasco. That's Alonzo."

The Black Fonz.

My heart *does* pump fear.

kenya

The Green Mile, *The Green Mile,* that was all I could think.

Alonzo seemed like he was as big as Michael Clarke Duncan.

Nowhere near as gentle, though.

He said, "Get out."

I looked out the window. It was completely dark out. Mama would be worried.

"Get out, Kenya."

I asked, "Do I have to?"

Alonzo flashed me a smile. "I'm not gonna hurt you. It's gonna be fine. We'll have some fun and then I'll get you home to your nerd brother."

I'd never thought I'd say such a thing, but at that moment I really missed Eric. I'd have given anything to touch his hand, hug his neck and tell him I loved him. He was corny, for sure. But he was my brother. And he loved me even when I didn't deserve his love. I felt sad all of a sudden. Sad and lonely. Sad and alone.

Alonzo's voice boomed, "I'm not playing, Kenya. Get out."

I said, "This some kind of warehouse?" I was stalling as best I could.

"This is a playground, Kenya. This is a place for Daddy and his little girl to play." Alonzo laughed. It was a horror-movie laugh, one I figured I'd never forget.

I asked, "And what about Fiasco?"

Alonzo shrugged. "Two's company, Kenya," he said, "and three's a crowd."

ERIC

"GET in, baby boy."

Mya pulls away from the curb down the street from my place before I can close the door all the way. I did the movie thing, stuffed pillows in my bed to approximate my size. If Mama checks in on me, hopefully she will be fooled.

I say, "The Black Fonz scares me."

Mya says, "Who?"

"Alonzo," I answer.

A cloud comes over her face. "He's dangerous. He's unstable."

"You noticed, too?"

"I know," Mya says. "I know."

"I saw him take two young girls in a room at the warehouse the other day. The room is marked PRIVATE. The way he touched them when he walked in behind them was terrible. I've been thinking about it ever since. I even had dreams about it."

Mya says, "Old Spice."

I say, "What?"

She looks at me. I suddenly realize that she's crying. Her eyes look like fragile glass. I ask, "Are you okay?"

She shakes her head, bites her lip. "Alonzo was my mother's boyfriend after my father died."

"What?"

Her hands are jittery. I'm not sure she should be driving. But I can't help. I'm two years away from getting a license myself.

Mya says, "He came in my room at night. He was always lathered in Old Spice. To this day I can't stand the smell of the stuff."

Oh no.

Mya continues, "He's so big, you know?"

I nod. Don't say anything.

Mya's hands tap the steering wheel like it's a drum. "I was so ashamed."

I say, "Not your fault."

Mya shakes her head but says, "I know. But I always felt like I could have done something to stop it."

I ask, "How long?"

"Three years."

I close my eyes at that bit of news. If he could molest Mya for three years, what was he capable of doing to Kenya in one night? I shudder to think about it.

I ask, "Fiasco knows?"

Mya nods.

"Why keep him around, then?"

Mya says, "Fiasco's a star."

"I know."

She says, "A celebrity."

"Yes."

"Tabloids pay a wad of cash for skeletons in a celebrity's closet."

I get it. I say, "To protect you."

Her shoulders bounce with her tears.

Fiasco comes bounding out of the mansion on Crawford's Corner Road. He moves over to the driver's side of Mya's Range Rover. They embrace briefly. Then Mya slides over next to me. Fiasco takes the wheel. He looks over at me, and then reaches out with his hand. At first I think it's for a handshake, then I realize he's handing me something. I take it. Heft it. It's the tire iron from the music video. The X-Treme didn't think I needed it. Overkill, he said. Well, I do need it.

I ask, "Where you think he took her?"

Fiasco looks at me with sadness.

He doesn't even have to answer.

I know the answer.

The warehouse.

kenya

I said, "I don't want to go in there."

Alonzo didn't seem to care what I wanted. He shoved me into the room marked PRIVATE. It was different than the rest of the place. Like a star's dressing room with all the amenities of comfort. A plush purple couch with a royal vibe to it took up one corner. A flat-screen plasma television set held down another corner. Large speakers hung from the ceiling. Candlelight was the only reprieve from pure darkness. Alonzo's face really took on the look of the devil in the glow of lights. I did my best not to look at him. Closed my eyes and pretended I was somewhere else.

"You like the place, baby girl?"

I didn't answer at first, and then I felt his hand on my wrist. I opened my eyes and smiled at him. My best opportunity to get out the situation unscathed, I figured, was to play along as much as possible, hope someone came in and spoiled the fun, hope he had a change of heart, hope for something.

I smiled at Alonzo. "It is beautiful. I didn't get to see much out there. Why don't you show me around?"

He said, "Later. After we've had our fun in here, I'll show you the entire place. Now, why don't you get comfortable? Take off that hot dress."

I had on a baby-doll dress the color of the North Carolina Tar Heels. It was a soft and sheer material. Not hot at all.

I asked Alonzo, "I could use a drink. That would make me comfortable."

He didn't answer, but I noticed a punch bowl in the corner. I went over to it.

It was filled with condoms.

Behind me I heard Alonzo's booming horror-movie laugh.

I closed my eyes again.

Eric

I look at the warehouse. A black Land Rover is parked at a hurried angle just in front.

Fiasco says, "He's here."

Mya says, "Three versus one."

I say, "Four. Kenya's a fighter."

We exit Mya's Range Rover.

Fiasco is in the lead, I'm right behind him, and Mya brings up the rear.

I say, "Bet I know where he has her."

Mya says, "That room marked PRIVATE you mentioned?"

I nod. Fiasco opens the front door with a key. We step into darkness. Fiasco doesn't hesitate, doesn't look for lights, just moves forward with a purpose. I'm sure his heart doesn't pump fear. Mine doesn't anymore, either. Kenya needs me. There is no time, or place, for fear. I hit the tire iron against my palm. I have a feel for its weight. It's definitely a weapon now.

We reach the PRIVATE room. A light leaks out at the bottom of the door. Fiasco turns the knob; the door eases open. Fiasco steps in, then I do, and then Mya. Alonzo has Kenya pinned in a corner, his back to us. Fiasco calls his name. I move forward, stand next to my favorite rapper. Mya stands next to me. Alonzo turns slowly. His face registers surprise for a moment. Then his mouth turns up in a smile. Just behind him Kenya smiles, too. She's okay, I realize. She's grateful we're here. We must have gotten here in time.

Alonzo says, "The whole family is here. Well, good."

I whisper to Fiasco, "You take his body. I've got his legs."

Fiasco nods.

We move forward.